# MIDDLE
# CHILD

## BUILD A FENCE ALL AROUND ME

### A Novel

## Taj Shotwell

# TAJ SHOTWELL PRODUCTIONS, LLC

**Middle Child:** Build A Fence All Around Me

Library of Congress Copyright © 2014 by Taj Shotwell.

ISBN-10: 0692351019
ISBN-13: 978-0-692-35101-7
**Author: Taj Shotwell**
> Website: **www.tajshotwell.com**
> Email: taj.shotwell@outlook.com

Self Publisher: Taj Shotwell

Cover Design: Taj Shotwell
Cover Graphics: Fiverr Webmark

Printed in the United States of America

*This is a work of* **_fiction and adult language_** *is used. Any references or similarities to actual events, real people, living or dead, or to real locales are intended to give the novel a sense of reality. Any similarity in other names, characters, places, and incidents, is entirely coincidental.*

*In Loving Memory of*

*Godfrey Fulton James (1914-1996)*
*and*
*Maggie Ella Douglass James (1920-2009)*

# Acknowledgements

*First, I give honor and thanks to God for my talents that he bestowed me. My deepest gratitude and appreciation to my lifelong and dearest friends and editors, Fatmah Saidah Radovich, from Costa Rica; and Betty Burston, a novelist and educator from California; for their unwavering love, encouragement, and diligence in editing this project. Special thanks to novelist, Ronald Gray, from Maryland, for his guidance in the world of publishing, marketing and distribution; and to Steven Gwin, from Florida, for his reviews.*

*Furthermore, I give thanks to the staff at My Provider Productions LLC and its affiliate, Black Wall Street New Dream Publishing, for their direction and trust in my work.*

*Finally, to my loving brother, Harold James, from Reno Nevada, who offered spiritual embracement; and to my relatives and friends who showed love and encouragement: thank you.*

# Prologue

*Life is for Living*

March 1, 2014, was a gleaming, almost spring day in the southern college town, turned city of Tallahassee, Florida; Annie Fowler Hightower sat alone in her living room staring reflectively out of the open plate-glass window that merged the beauty of her backyard with that of her pristine and sparkly white living room. Surrounded by the splendor of paintings, sculptures, and artifacts; both old and new; Annie pondered the life she had grown and shaped; and the past into which she has been placed by the design of the universe.

Glancing upwards and outwards from her reveries, she saw her image captured in the odd-shaped mirror from some country included among the destinations of her much traveled world.

"Sixty four years of age… I can't believe it," whispered her heart to her mind as she reflected on the long and difficult journey that had led her to this day, time and place; her 64th birthday.

Rising with the agility of a woman thirty years her junior, she walked past the recently taken photo of her shapely body in a bikini, walked across the room, and gently sat in a side chair- her favorite spot since her early retirement from a local university. Almost absent-mindedly, she lifted a family photo album from the stack that rested on the floor, looked down, and quickly opened the cover.

As she turned the pages of the photo album in her lap, her eyes focused on a photo of her family taken in 1951. Her 36 year old father, Sgt. Jessie Jacob Fowler, stood handsome and proud in his military uniform. Standing next to him was her beautiful mother, Margret Elaine McGwin, who was her father's junior by six years. In front of them were their six children. Standing were her oldest sister, Elaine, who was nine years old, and her brother, Jessie, Jr., who was seven. Also standing, in front of the two oldest children, were Samantha, age 4 and Robert Lee, 3 years of age. Finally, seated on a bench were Claudine at 2 years old, and the sixth child, Annie, who was only one year old.

Staring at her miniature reflection, Annie could internally see and hear the family stories told by her mother and relatives over the years. Indeed, her actual experiences growing up ran before her. As she stared at the photo, she wondered why her Daddy and Mother hadn't stopped at six children. To her, this was a perfect portrait of a family.

2

Annie then randomly lifted another photo from the stack dated 1970. It displayed the images of five additional siblings, who had been added to the family portrait after her own birth. Three years after Annie's birth, Donny arrived. Then, two years later, Daisy was born. Four years later Aaron arrived and within three years, two more girls, Janis and Martha, were born.

Finally, the Fowler Family was completed, totaling, eleven children - four boys and seven girls. This officially made Annie the middle child.

Suddenly, Annie's phone began to ring. Despite the piercing noise, her eyes remained upon the family portrait and the web of memories which the images spun in her mind.

# CHAPTER 1

*Up, Up and Away*

Annie's father, Jessie Jacob Fowler, was born in Collierville, Tennessee, in 1914. Jessie's father, Jacob Fowler, was a carpenter and his mother, Candice Fairweather Fowler, was a homemaker. Jessie had two younger brothers named Jason and John. When he was a young boy, his parents left the country town to move to the city of Memphis; but, due to the pressures of city life they soon divorced. Jessie and his brothers worked with their father in construction. Jessie learned the carpentry skills like his father; while his youngest brother, John, learned masonry, and his middle brother, Jason, became a skilled painter. Jessie completed the tenth grade, then worked with CCC Camp for several years, worked with his father, and in 1946 joined the Army. He was a noticeably handsome man, with large brown eyes and the greatest smile that drew attention. His tightly kinky hair was always cut and groomed to perfection. Jessie's paper sack complexion was a combination of African and Native American genetics. He was very vain about maintaining a muscular body. At six feet tall, Jessie showed off his broad shoulders and narrow waist.

In the summer of 1937, Jessie was on leave from the U.S. CCC Camp (Civilian Conservation Corps), Jessie visited his best friend, Gordon, in Germantown, Tennessee and he was Jessie's work buddy and comrade-in-arms. They attended a local church service. In the choir, singing "How Great Thou Art" with passion, was lovely, seventeen year old, Margaret Elaine McGwin. She belted out a high C that immediately caught Jessie's attention. The decision was made. Jessie had finally met the woman who would become his wife. For the rest of the service, Jessie, mesmerized by Margaret's beauty; he simply sat and stared.

Margaret stood five feet five inches; she had long silky dark curls that fell to her waist, the cutest freckles Jessie had ever seen, and a gorgeous light, creamy, olive complexion that she inherited from her African, Scott-Irish, and Native American ancestry. As Margaret moved from the choir loft down to a pew, Jessie noticed that she had a shapely body and nice legs that turned his head, as well as the heads of other men in the church.

Jessie couldn't wait until after the service was over so that he could make his move.

"May the Lord go with Thee......," Pastor Stewart finally said after a long benediction. Jessie, hopeful of capturing Margaret's attention, quickly stood and looked around.

"Damn, that woman is too 'fyne' for her own good," thought Jessie as Margaret leaned down in the consultation with the pianist regarding a song she was scheduled to sing at the 3'oclock service. It was the day of the Pastor's anniversary and members of other Christian Methodist Episcopal churches would be arriving shortly. The sisters were setting up tables with all sorts of goodies under a grove of bees in the rear of the church.

Jessie hadn't planned to stay for the afternoon event, but quickly changed his mind as he smelled the ribs barbequing on the grill. But, it wasn't, of course, only the promise of some good eating to come that made Jessie hesitant to leave.

"Hey Man, we getting out of here or what?" Gordon asked.

"Well, why don't we stay for the afternoon service," Jessie asked as his eyes still focused upon Margaret.

Following Jessie's eyes, Gordon smiled with understanding.

"I'll stay only if she's got a sister."
"Okay, then let's find out," said Jessie
with a twinkle in his eye.

Before Gordon could respond, Jessie had
rushed from his side and was talking to a woman
who appeared to be in her late sixties. Gordon
walked over and joined in the conversation.

"Hi, I'm Gordon Walker," he said as he
reached out his hand to Ms. Rosie, the lady
who Jessie had chosen as his primary source of
information. The extensive conversation
revealed that Jessie had made the perfect
choice.

Jessie and Gordon learned from Ms. Rosie
that Margaret was the fourth child of eleven
children: of whom seven were girls. Gordon was
excited to hear this information. Margaret's
family was well-known in the local communities
for their musical skills and ministries. Her
father was the church's pastor. Margaret's
mother sang and played the piano. Her mother
also made additional income as a seamstress.

"That girl is going to make some lucky
man a good wife… she can cook real good too,"
Ms. Rosie lowered her voice.

"She made most of her clothes. She looks
sharp all the time."

Jessie was very impressed with the dress that Margaret was wearing.

Margaret had other attributes that Ms. Rose had not shared with the guys; Margaret was strictly a country girl. She worked hard harvesting with her family to gather and preserve food for the large family. While not allowed in the family home, she enjoyed dancing. Margaret was also smart. Although, high school diplomas were not offered at the schools during that time, Margaret completed the eleven years that were offered.

Ms. Rosie continued her monologue as Jessie and Gordon escorted her to a table. By the end of the day, Jessie knew that Margaret was the girl he was going to marry.

What Jessie didn't know on that fateful day was that Margaret had noticed him as soon as he had walked through those church doors.
Furthermore, she had told herself, "That is my husband". Sure enough, one year later they were married.

Jessie and Margaret were inseparable and traveled together everywhere the CCC Camp would allow them. They had a honeymoon that lasted over five years before the first child was born.

When Margret became pregnant, they settled in Memphis and in 1943 bought a new

**8**

home in the town of Orange Mound. Today it is a historical town. The first born was, Elaine. She was a gorgeous baby and looked much like her father. She was very girly and proper. Each word was enunciated as she spoke. She learned to sew and how to style hair. Elaine was always properly dressed and her hair and nails were maintained. She was Daddy's girl.

Although, Margaret was a country girl, she insisted that her children call her, "Mother". The best Elaine could do was to call her 'Mur'.

Two years later and still in Memphis, Jessie and Marget welcome the birth of their first son. The cute little boy was named after Jessie, but was nick named Junior. He who kept these traits into manhood. However, he did not show much respect towards girls.

Jessie continued to work for the CCC Camp until it ended in 1942. After 1942 Jessie worked with his father and brothers as a carpenter until 1946 when he joined the army was deployed to Virgina for four years between Ft. Eustis and Ft. Monroe. Jessie took his wife and two children with him.

Jessie, truly a family man, did not like being away from his wife and children. He also had a close relationship with his mother.

9

Jessie always provided for his family and mother; and played an active part in the lives of his children as they were growing up.

In Virgina, they lived in military housing. Four more children were born during their stay in Virgina.

The third born was Samantha, who was a lovely baby with very thin straight hair. A gentle soul and would give another the clothes off her back. She also allowed people to misuse her. Samantha loved to laugh and showed off her dance moves.

The fourth born was Robert Lee, a handsome care free child and man. He showed no concerns regarding what was going on around him and he didn't like to share. He called himself, "Pretty Boy" and had inherited a good singing voice from his mother and his father's complexion. He grew up popular with the girls.

Claudine, the fifth child, was born eleven months after Robert Lee. She was a healthy, cute baby with thick wavy hair. Claudine was shy and sly when dealing with other family members. She didn't speak much, but continually found ways to undermine a few of her siblings.

The sixth child, Annie, was a small baby at birth. Unlike the others, she had a full head of kinky golden-reddish hair. She was an independent tom-boy and would try almost anything. Yet, she was a Daddy's girl, and was teased by her siblings for sucking her thumb. A couple of days after Margaret brought Annie home from the hospital, six year old Junior forced a penny in baby Annie's mouth.

"I told you not to bring no mo' guls home- - too many guls," Junior shouted at his mother. Margaret reached Annie just in time as she began to choke on the coin planted in her mouth by Junior.

Jessie and Margret surprised their relatives when they brought back six children home when they only had two when they had left Memphis.

Two years later, Jessie was deported to Korea. Margaret and the children remained in Memphis. Shortly after Jessie returned to Memphis, a cute baby, Donny, was born with beautiful curly hair. He didn't smile much and cried all the time. As a child and teen, he was very shy and needed attention.

Jessie had developed PTSD during his Korean experience. Maggie dealt with his abusiveness for many years.

After Margaret recovered from the child birth of Donny, Jessie packed up the family, and with all seven children flew to Europe; where he was stationed for over three years in

Germany. During that time, the eighth child
was born in Germany named Daisy. She was a cute
bouncy, happy baby girl with thick curly hair.
Yet, even as a little girl, she was stubborn
and had to be in control of everything. She
enjoyed being the life of the party, but at
the same time, if there was any sibling
rivalry, Daisy was usually the one in the
center of it. She too had inherited Margaret's
ability to sing.

While still in Europe, Jessie was ordered
to return to the United States for duty in
Missouri. Finding housing for ten people was a
challenge for the government at that time. As
a result, Jessie packed up the eight children
and returned to Memphis where Margaret and the
children lived until about a year later when a
four bedroom duplex finally became available
on the military base.

The trip to Missouri was quite different
than any other travel. All ten members of the
family squeezed into a large Ford station-
wagon. Jessie, Margaret, and the two youngest
-Donny and Daisy- sat in the front seats. In
the wide rear seat were Elaine, Samantha,
Claudine, and Annie. Riding in the storage area
in the far rear of the car were Junior and
Robert Lee. Packed food and water were placed
beneath the seats.

The roof of the car was loaded with suitcases and because there was no air conditioning, all windows were down. As they started the six hour trip to Ft. Leonard Wood, Missouri, it resembled the "Hillbillies" moving to Hollywood; and like the TV show, Beverly Hillbillies, the journey became an extension of the family happiness.

Once settled into the new base, Jessie was placed in charge of the mess hall. This was ideal for his large family. During his tenure in this position the government had very little wasted food because Jessie did not throw away any leftovers. He kept his family well-fed and healthy.

In the mornings, the children were awakened with the choice of cereal, fresh juice, eggs, bacon, sausage, milk, and cocoa. For dinner there were plenty of meats, fresh vegetables and breads.

Three years after arriving in Missouri, the ninth child was born; an eleven pound baby boy was named Aaron. He was an easy going baby and didn't cry much. He was always eager to please others and didn't speak much. But, Aaron loved to play little tricks on his siblings.

Jessie was proud of his wonderful family and loved taking photos of everyone. After Aaron was born in 1959, Jessie purchased an

8mm movie camera that recorded only black and white movies without audio. Every family gathering and holiday, Jessie had the camera ready. Some time afterwards, the family would sit down to watch the movies with homemade popcorn and lemonade; and occasionally Elaine would make homemade caramel to pour over the popcorn and homemade donuts. During the movie, the family would laugh and chat. Although they couldn't hear what was said on the move; they knew exactly what had been said. One film showed Margaret dancing up a storm. She was turning and kicking her legs. Margaret looked stunning. Yes, Jessie was sentimental and loved to keep wonderful memories of his family.

While still in Missouri, Jessie took leave time, and with assistance from his father, they added a room to the Memphis home for his mother. His youngest brother had already taken in their elderly father. When the room was finished, Jessie's mother lived in the rear of the home while other renters occupied the front section. The renters lived there while the family was away for long periods of time.

Throughout Jessie and Margaret's marriage, they had opened their home to families in need. It was hard to imagine with all of the people living in the house, how they always managed to find space for another relative or friend to stay; but they did. Some stayed for a short period time and others stayed longer.

When Jessie and his family were living in Virginia, he allowed both of his brothers and their families to stay in the Memphis house. His brothers agreed to pay the $60 monthly mortgage. Within a year, Jessie received a notice for foreclosure on his house. Those were difficult times for a lot of people. His brothers had not paid the mortgage for three months. Jessie took a leave of absence to return to Memphis to refinance the house and to make arrangements for his brothers to move out of the house. Jessie was able to save his home without telling Margaret about the incident. It would be more than twenty years later when she accidently came across the mortgage files, but Margaret never mentioned her discovery to Jessie.

After Jessie's four year duty in Missouri, Jessie accepted an exciting opportunity in Ft. Braggs, North Carolina, as an Army Airborne paratrooper. He was required to report to duty immediately for a two year assignment. Jessie made the decision to retire after this particular duty was completed, thereby, ending a twenty seven year career in the Army.

Jessie and Margaret thought it would be best to relocate the family back to Memphis instead of North Carolina. Stability had become particularly important, since the three oldest children were in high school. They felt the environment would be more familiar and the children would not have to experience another adjustment making and then leaving more friends. Margaret was pregnant during the move and a few months later the tenth child, a lovely baby girl, Janis, was born. Janis was also a quiet baby, but soon claimed her voice and became very loud. She was outgoing and loved to make people happy.

It was a blessing for the children to have their paternal grandmother, "Granny", living with them. Each child had their own special bond with her.

Approximately ten months later, the eleventh and final baby girl was born. She was named Martha. She was a sweet and adorable baby who always had a smile on her face. Martha loved being around people and craved attention.

In 1963, Jessie retired from the Army and returned to Memphis. He worked a few years at the VA hospital, but very soon entered into a true retirement. Jessie and Margaret parented eleven endearing children. These memories tell Annie's story.

## CHAPTER 2

*Early Memories*

Early one morning in Germany, Annie was in the kitchen helping her oldest sister Elaine, make maple syrup for the pancakes that would be prepared for breakfast. Her mother, Margaret, had turned on the radio to the "Arthur Godfrey Show". Annie, shaking her head to the beat of the rock 'n' roll song "Li'l Girl, Li'l Girl" by Donnie Boyd, that was playing on the radio, pushed a chair to the edge of the stove and climbed aboard. The pot steamed as she watched Elaine stir the syrup until it thickened. Annie wanted to help stir.

"Annie don't you get too close to that stove -you might get burned," she heard her mother's warning.

"Yes Ma'am" Annie always answered. Just as she moved even closer to the stove, Annie heard her mother yell out.

"Heidi! Heidi! Where is that lazy girl? Annie git down and go knock on her door and tell her I want her." Annie got down, ran to the rear of the home, and knocked on Heidi's door.

"Heidi, mother wants you." There was no answer. Annie knocked again.

"Heidi... Heiiiiidiiiii, mother wants you," she yelled still in a child's voice. "Ok, Ok, I come!" Heidi finally answered.

It was the year 1956 and the place was Stuttgart, Germany. Heidi was an eighteen year old German woman who had been hired by the German government as a live-in maid. She was assigned to work in the home of the United States Army Sgt. Jessie Fowler. The Fowlers had lived in different parts of Germany for more than three years. Margaret was thankful for the extra help in housekeeping, especially with eight children. Margaret appreciated the irony of having a German maid clean the home of a Negro family. This she knew would never happen in the racist country into which she was born or in Hitler's Germany.

Jessie had orders to return to the States. In fact, on that very day a photographer was scheduled to take family portraits. Jessie, Margaret and the children had had a good experience in Germany and, as a result, didn't mind the elderly German woman and the two German boys, seven and twelve years old, who would be a part of the photo shoot in order to show good relations between Germany and the USA.

When Annie ran back to the kitchen, Jessie, Margaret and her siblings had sat down to eat. Annie wanted to pour her own syrup, so, she stood on the chair next to the stove and stuck a spoon into the hot pot. Suddenly she squealed; Annie had burned her hand, but wouldn't cry because she thought she would get in trouble. The second degree burn left a life time scar on her hand as a reminder and a souvenir from Germany.

Later that day, Annie took her place standing next to her father, Jessie, as she said, "cheese." But, even at sixty four, Annie often found herself viewing that scar and remembering with fondness a scar of pain that over the years became a symbolic of the love shared by her family during the early dawn of her life.

# CHAPTER 3

### USA

While life in Germany had its own lessons, other childhood experiences also taught Annie about familiar love, and pain.

The Fowler's Memphis home was built off the ground; held by large brick stilts that left a two foot space between the house and the ground, there was enough space for a small child to crawl under. Annie loved to play under the house. On some hot days, she found a cool spot and took naps. On one bright, humid day, Annie heard her mother call to her. She rushed across the crawl space on her knees. Suddenly, she felt a sharp pain in her left knee. Looking down, she saw blood and sticking from her knee were two large pieces of glass. Annie needed help from her mother.

"Mother-r-r!" she called repeatedly. Her mother standing by the kitchen sink did not hear Annie's call. Annie, now quite panicked, called again. Hearing a noise, Margaret turned from her sink full of dishes and walked slowly through the house. She was about to dismiss the perception when Annie called again, "Mooooother-r-r-r." Margaret rushed outside; crawled under the house and pulled Annie into the yard. She lifted Annie and carried her into the house where she removed the glass; cleaned and bandaged Annie's wound.

"You are a little girl- not a boy; never ever go under that house again," Margaret, in tears, scolded.

The scars left another life-time reminder of her carelessness. Annie followed her mother' advice and never went under the house again, but it didn't stop her from climbing trees.

Early one Saturday morning, Annie was awakened by loud noises. She heard a voice and heavy tapping on the street.

"Iiiccce Man. Iiiccce Man."

Annie jumped out of the bed and ran to the front window. When she pulled back the curtain she couldn't believe her eyes. There, parked in front of the house was a man sitting on a wagon with a horse. Moments later Annie noticed that a couple of her siblings were also watching. They watched the man step off the wagon and walked to the back of it. He pulled back a large cloth that covered the entire wagon. He pulled out the large medal ice tongs and lifted a large block of ice. The man carried it down the driveway to the rear of the house and into the kitchen where Margaret was waiting. The kids ran to the kitchen just in time to watch the man insert the block of

**21**

ice into the icebox through its special door. Annie learned that the ice would be delivered on a regular basis to keep the food cold. The children followed the iceman to his wagon where he gave each child some ice chips. Annie had never seen real horses before, just those on her favorite TV shows. It was a good day for Annie.

It was not long after that day, on a warm morning, while Annie was sitting on the lower branch of the tree in front of the house; she heard unusual noises coming toward the house. She wasn't sure in what direction the noise was coming from.

"Raaagg Man….. Raaagg Man."

Annie quickly turned to the voice she heard. She was amazed to see a man driving a horse and wagon. The wagon was filled with all sorts of cloths and clothes. Margaret came out the door with a few clothing items and a large jar of water in her hands. She stepped down the stairs onto the driveway and walked to the edge of the street. Annie climbed down from the tree, but stayed a distance and observed.

"Hole gal," the man commanded his horse. The horse stopped and the sweaty old colored man, with a slim body, stepped down from his wagon and greeted Margaret.

"Gud Mo'nin Ma'am."

"Good morning Sir. Here are some rags and you must be thirsty on this warm morning," Margaret said.

He took the rags and threw them in the wagon.

"Yes Ma'am, thank ya so much, I really do pre'shait it."

He took the water from Margaret, and drank the entire 32 ounces. She offered him more, but he declined. He climbed up on the wagon, sat down, and reached for his reigns. He nodded his head to Margaret and Annie.

"Git up," he commanded the horse.

"Raaagg Man. Raaagg Man."

Annie watched as the horse trotted down the street until they disappeared. She learned that the "Rag Man" sold rags, but he also accepted donations of rags. The most important lesson she learned that morning, was to be kind and respectful to all people. She also hoped she would not be told to pick up the big present that the horse left behind on the street in front of the house.

One day, Annie had spent most of the late afternoon outside playing with a neighborhood friend and climbing the tree. Finally tired, she went inside the house. She heard her mother, who was in the kitchen, singing "Precious Lord".

"...I'm tired, I'm weak, Lord I'm worn;
Through the storm, through the night."

What Annie saw next was so confusing and painful that she froze at the sight of it. Her older sister Samantha, 3 years old, was sitting alone, on the sofa, with a swollen, shut eye and bruises on her face. Frightened, Annie looked around to find some reason for what she saw. Her younger brother, Donny, and her sister, Daisy, were asleep in the back bedroom. The older siblings had not come home yet. Jessie was home on leave, but had left the house.

Annie slowly walked over to her sister and sat beside her.

"Samantha, what happened to you?" she asked.

"Daddy hit me because I messed my pants at school. He had to pick me up from school," Samantha whispered.

Tearful, Annie held Samantha's hand and set with her in silence. Margaret continued to sing while she did her chores in the kitchen.

"Hear my cry, hear my call

Hold my hand lest I fall

Take my hand precious Lord,

**24**

Lead me home."

Shortly, after that experience, Annie began to wet the bed nearly every night. It was many years later when Annie understood the impact of that highly traumatic experience. The level of empathy demonstrated by Annie became a forever bond that allowed the two sisters to remain close.

Several months after the trauma occurred, the family moved to the military base in Ft. Leonard Wood, Missouri. It was only weeks before school was to start. The four bedroom duplex was nice and clean. A door was built to join the duplex as one large home. Jessie and Margaret had one bedroom. Elaine and Samantha shared a bedroom. Junior, Robert Lee, and Donny shared a bedroom with bunk beds. The last bedroom, also with bunk beds, was shared by Claudine, Annie and Daisy. One of the living rooms, known as the "front-room", was strictly for Jessie's and Margaret's entertainment space.

Annie was excited about starting school. The night before she laid out her clothes and helped her Mother make sandwiches. A little later, Margaret sat Annie down in front of the stove to press her hair. Earlier she had washed and twisted Annie's long kinky hair into eight little balls all over her head. Margaret

**25**

placed the straightening iron-comb on the eye of the stove to get it hot. Annie was very "tender-headed" and didn't like to get her hair combed or pressed. While the iron-comb was heating, Margaret began to comb out one of the balls. Annie squealed, placed her hands on her head and dodged the comb. Her mother popped Annie's hands with the comb in her hand. When Annie straightened up, Margaret picked up the hot iron-comb; wiped it on a cotton rag and commenced to press Annie's hair. Just the sight of the hot comb made Annie slide down in her chair onto the floor.

"Girl, get back up in this chair," Margaret yelled. She lifted Annie back into the chair. This went on for a while.

Finally, Margaret stood up, placed the hot iron-comb on a metal holder and walked away.

"That's okay, Annie. You can just stay home tomorrow," Margaret said as she paused at the door.

"I'll be good, Mother," Annie cried.

"Are you sure?" Margaret asked.

"I promise, Mother… I promise," Annie pleaded. That did it; Annie then closed her eyes and didn't move until her hair was finished.

Annie's sisters' hair didn't need as much maintenance as hers. Margaret would just add a little hair oil, then comb, brush and braid their hair. Margaret styled all the girls' hair similarly- with three braids; one braided on the top of their heads that hung on the side or in the back, and one braided on each side of their heads.

After Margaret completed combing the girls' hair, she called all the children into the kitchen. She opened the cabinet door and pulled out a large bottle of "Cod Liver Oil". It was time for the periodic health remedy that the children dreaded. No one wanted to be the first in line.

"You guys better get over here now!" Margaret told them. Annie didn't want to, but, she jumped in front of the line. Margaret poured the oil in a tablespoon.

"Open your mouth wide."

Annie opened her mouth as wide as she could. Margaret had done this so often that she could pour the oil straight into each child's mouth without the spoon touching their lips. This kept her from having to use different spoons.

"Now swallow." Margret told her. Annie hated the taste, but she swallowed it; and

**27**

thought she was going to throw up. But, she didn't.

The last child stood before Margret as she poured the cod liver oil into his mouth.

"Okay. Did I miss anyone?" Margret asked. No one replied.

"Well next week you will get the "Sweet-tine.""

"Yuk…uhmmm, oh no," the kids reacted.

Another remedy that Annie and her siblings dreaded was for the prevention of lice and ring-worms. Each year, Margaret gave her children a teaspoon of turpentine with sugar; she called it "Sweet-tine". Although this concoction had been controversial in the medical arena, none of her children had ever been infested with lice or ring-worms.

Annie had a wonderful experience in school on that next day. She met a cute little blond-haired girl with green eyes whose name was Susan. They became best friends even though Black people lived on one side of the military base and the white families on the other side but they lived only a couple of streets apart and they met sometimes in the park near their homes. They remained friends for the duration of Jessie's Missouri assignment. Her friendship with Susan taught her that because of the military life style, friends would come and go. When Annie's family moved back to Memphis, she never saw Susan again.

By the third grade in Fort Lenard Wood, Annie's teacher recommended that she receive speech therapy. Annie had difficulty pronouncing words beginning with "S" and "Th". Learning new things was always exciting to Annie, and she looked forward to the weekly one hour sessions with a very nice teacher named, Miss Rooks. Annie continued the sessions for the entire school year and completed with satisfaction. Annie's speech impairment was cured.

When Annie was a little older, she came home from school and noticed her mother removing a stripe from her father's uniform before she pressed the shirt. She was a little confused, but didn't ask any questions at that time.   About six months later Annie saw her mother putting that strip back on her father's uniform and pressing it.

"Why do you take it off and then put it on?" curious Annie, finally asked her mother.

"Well, sometimes people make mistakes and then they make up for it," Margaret explained.

"Did Daddy make a mistake?" Annie asked.

"Yes," said Margaret.

**29**

"And he made up for it?" asked Annie.

"Yes he did," Margaret replied.

Young Annie seemed satisfied with the answer at the time. However, about a year later Annie saw her mother again taking off a strip. It was many years later when Annie truly understood.

# CHAPTER 4

## *Summer Travel*

Each summer Jessie drove the family to Memphis for a visit. The entire family would stay for about two weeks. Jessie and Margaret decided to let Annie and Claudine stay with their grandmother through the end of the summer break. Because they were only thirteen months apart in age, they were sometimes referred to as "The Twins". Annie and Claudine, excited by the promise of an extended stay with Granny, Candice Fairweather Fowler, began planning their activities for the duration of their stay.

Annie and Claudine agreed to visit their first cousins from both sides of the family. One of their favorite outings, each summer, was with Jessie's youngest brother, Uncle John's   family, who lived on two streets south of their home. John's loving wife, Aunt Daisy, enjoyed all her nieces. Annie's younger sister Daisy was name after their aunt.  Aunt Daisy took her six children and her two nieces to the annual state fair. Tuesday was the only day that Colored people could attend the fair. They spent the entire day enjoying the rides and eating ice cream.

A young girl who lived in the neighborhood was the same age as Annie. Her name was Carmela and she was a little tinier than Annie. Carmela lived on a street only a block away. Each summer thereafter, Annie and Carmela found fun activities to do. Annie and Carmela became lifelong friends and referred to each other as cousins. Their friendship led to another learning experience.

One day Annie, Claudine, and Carmela were out playing at Carmela's house. It was almost sundown.

"It's time to go home," Claudine told Annie.

"No, let's stay a little longer," Annie insisted.

"You know Granny will whip us if we don't get home before dark." Claudine said.

"No she won't. You know she's too old to whip us," Annie laughed.

"You better come on," Claudine ordered. Annie unwillingly followed Claudine home. They walked to the back of the house to Granny's bedroom door entrance. Claudine went inside and Annie sat outside on the door steps.

"Annie come on in and get ready for bed." Granny called out a few minutes later.

"Yes, Ma'am," Annie said as she walked into Granny room and towards the girls' bed room.

"So you think I'm too old to whip yall, uh?" Granny said.

Speechless and embarrassed, Annie quickly closed the bedroom door behind her.

That experience taught Annie to never underestimate anyone and to never speak derisively of another person.

## CHAPTER 5

*More Life's Lessons*

Indeed Annie quickly learned other life lessons. She learned her first lesson regarding life's threat to women of all ages.

One night, when Annie was about nine years old, she had gone to bed. In the upper bunk bed, Claudine was sleeping. In the bed across from Annie, Daisy slept. Annie was on the lower bunk in a deep sleep lying on her side facing Daisy, with her thumb in her mouth. Sometime during the night, Annie felt a cool breeze on her body and realized that her brother, Junior, who was 15 years old, was in the bed with her. She did not move. He was lying facing her backside with his back against the wall. Annie still did not move. She was confused as to why he was in her bed, but was too frightened to move. Junior began to lower Annie's panties. Annie stiffened up. Slowly and quietly he lowered her panties below her bottom. The next thing Annie felt something like a pencil with an eraser moving up and down her buttocks. That went on for a few minutes and then there was a poking movement on the same spot of her butt. This went on for another few minutes. And then it was over. Junior pulled Annie panties back up, climbed out of the bed and left. Annie was in shock. She

**34**

didn't understand what had happened, yet felt
it wasn't right.

Margaret and Jessie did not have the
skills to talk to their children about sex,
menstrual periods, dating, love or anything
dealing with the opposite sex. Therefore, they
made no attempts. They didn't know it then,
but those major weaknesses had a colossal
affect on their children's lives as they grew
up.

After the third visit from Junior in her
bedroom, Annie decided to tell someone. She
had always looked up to and respected her
oldest sister Elaine. To Annie, Elaine was the
perfect lady and trusted her. Elaine was
seventeen years old at the time. And on the
next day, Annie caught Elaine alone watching
TV in the living room. She walked up to
Elaine.

"Elaine, Junior comes in my room at night
and pulls my panties down, I don't like it."

Elaine gave Annie a quick look.

"Why are you telling me? You better tell
Mother or someone else," she yelled. Elaine
continued to watch TV. This was more than a
nine year old could handle. Annie ran back to
her bedroom and shut the door. She felt ashamed
and thought she had done something wrong. She
didn't feel safe. Annie never spoke of it

again. She did, however, stay awake a few nights, laid her back against the wall, and her bed wetting worsened. Soon, Junior stopped coming into Annie's bedroom.

Little Annie had already learned from her family that public crying was not an acceptable reaction, so she only cried when she was alone. In addition, this experience taught her that asking for help was a sign of weakness and she would have to take care of her own problems.

About a few months later, seventeen year old Elaine gave birth to a cute baby girl. This was Jessie's and Margaret's first grandchild.

For ten years Annie's siblings teased and bullied her about bed-wetting and sucking her thumb. Her siblings would place hot sauce on her thumb at night and they nick-named her, "Sucka-Thumb-Bull-Frog", As a result of her bed-wetting, they called her "Pee Pot". Annie also bit her nails, but that seemed to escape criticism from anyone.

Then only ten years of age, Annie had decided to stop sucking her thumb. One night, just before bed time, she removed a string from her shoe. She used the string to tie her right thumb to the bunk bed pole. She then laid on her side and eventually fell asleep. The next morning Annie woke up refreshed. Most importantly no thumb in her month. Better yet, she had no cravings during the day for her thumb. Annie never sucked her thumb again.

The bed wetting was a totally different issue. It would take a couple of years before that matter would be resolved.

One evening Jessie and Margaret loaded all the children into the station wagon and went out to the soldier's club. There were other families there, and only a few other children present. Jessie's children had been to the club before. On this particular evening, Jessie and some of his army buddies had arranged to get together for Jessie's farewell. He was leaving Ft. Leonard Wood, MO and being transferred to Ft. Bragg, NC.

Jessie had the most children there; and of course, his children were the best behaved. Long tables were set up in a huge room. Everyone sat down while slow blues type music was being played by a live band. A few people got up to dance. The adults drank alcohol; while Margaret and the kids had sodas. Margaret knew she would be the designated driver for the night. There was a lot of food: chicken, steaks, ham, vegetables, rolls and desserts.

Shortly after everyone had been served and had eaten, the band played faster music such as, "Cadillac Baby", by Roy Brown; "Oh Babe", by Wynonie Harris and "I'm Going to Have Myself a Ball", by Tiny Bradshaw.

Jessie grabbed Margaret's hand and led her to the dance floor. He turned her around; they kicked up their legs; and shook their heads. Samantha got up to dance and Annie followed. Soon the dance floor was full. Everyone was laughing and having fun. Jessie and Margaret were happy. When Jessie came back to the table, he hugged and kissed his children and soon headed back to the dance floor. Annie remembered his wet kiss on her check.

It was a wonderful celebration of the end of one journey and the beginning of many journeys to come.

# CHAPTER 6

*Transitioning*

The Fowler family returned to Memphis in 1961. Margaret was about ready to give birth to Janis. While still in the military, Jessie had to leave immediately for his last duty in North Carolina.

For about a year there were a total of fourteen family members living in a four bedroom house that had only one bathroom. Since Granny had one bedroom, and Margaret and Jessie had the second bedroom, the remaining two bedrooms were shared among eleven children. Rolling beds and cots were placed in the living room and dining room. There was little privacy and, as a result, tensions built between siblings, and between parents and children. After a year, Elaine married and moved with her baby to Oregon. Junior dropped out of high school and joined the Navy.

In addition, food wasn't as plentiful as it had been on the military base. The breakfast offerings consisted of fatback bacon, eggs and toast. There were no more milk deliveries. Instead, the canned and concentrated "Pet Milk" was watered down to make enough for the family. Sometimes there were cornflakes or rice with butter and sugar.

Other meals included bologna sandwiches, mayo sandwiches, and beans, greens with ham hocks, cornbread, pig's feet, ox tails, and chicken. Regardless, of the changed menu, the children were fed and they didn't complain.

Margaret took jobs sewing to earn income. And on weekends she took Annie or Claudine with her to clean houses and babysit for white people. Annie also had a little job washing dishes for neighbors. Samantha although pregnant, found odd jobs, to help the family. Robert Lee delivered newspapers.

"Hey Claudine and Annie, if yall help me deliver papers, I will pay yall at the end of the week, when I git paid."

For one week before going to school, Annie and Claudine got up at 4'clock to help deliver the papers. At the end of the week, Robert Lee received his pay. Claudine asked for her money and Robert Lee paid her. But when Annie asked for her money, Robert Lee told her he would pay her the next week. The next week came and Robert Lee refused to pay Annie. Annie was so hurt that she cried. She didn't tell her mother or anyone. This was another lesson Annie learned; that some people are users and takers.

The next year when Annie turned twelve years old, she learned another important lesson. Totally oblivious to the racial segregation and hatred that existed in the South, Jessie and Margaret, as with sex, had not prepared their children for the transition from life in the military bases to life in the South. The children had never been told about different races, color, segregation and the social issues in the south. Jessie and Margaret had never used the "N" word in front of their children. They never told their children that society looked upon them differently than other human beings.

Annie's experience since the family moved to Memphis had only been in the local community. The family's home was in a community that had hard working home owners who cared about their homes, yards, and their children. The yards were groomed, and the brick and wooden homes were always maintained. The streets were cleaned. The children were dressed properly and they respected adults. The neighbors knew each other and looked out for each other's children. It was an unofficial built-in neighborhood watch.

The neighborhood children walked to school. The neighbors sat out on their porches and greeted the children on their way to school and when they returned. When neighbors had cookouts, they shared their food with others. When a neighbor had financial problems there were helping hands. When the children did something wrong, they would sometimes get spanked by the neighbors as well as by their parents. Moreover, any dysfunctions that existed were kept in the privacy of the homes and not shown to the community.

When Annie learned her lessons on race, they came as quite a surprise.

"Junior? Junior?" called Margaret.

"Ma'am," Junior answered as he rushed in the kitchen where Margaret stood.

"Baby I need you to go down town and pay the electric bill, it must be paid today or it will be late," Margaret said in a panicked voice.

"Yes Ma'am," Junior answered.    Junior headed out the door.

"I want to go," Annie whispered in a soft voice.    Junior first stared at Annie and then at his mother.  Margaret nodded her head.

"Let's go" he said. Annie was ecstatic. Annie had never been downtown or on the city bus.  She recalled riding the school bus in Missouri, so she didn't think it would be any different. She was so excited to go on an errand with her big brother.

Junior and Annie stood at the bus stop until the bus arrived and the doors opened.

Junior jumped in first and Annie followed.
Junior paid the money and walked towards the
back.   Annie saw a front seat and sat down.
She had always sat in the front seat on the
school bus.

"Hello," she said to the bus driver, as
she always did. The bus driver looked back at
her and frowned.

"Boy, ya better come git this gull, and
take har on back wit ya," he yelled in a deep
southern accent.

Junior, rushed up, grabbed Annie's hand
and led her to the back of the bus.

"What did I do?" Annie asked.

"Hush, we have to sit in the back" Junior
whispered.

"But, why?" Annie, now disappointed,
asked.

"Because we are Colored," Junior said,
in a lower whisper.

"What is colored?" confused Annie asked.

Junior didn't answer.

They reached the utility company and got
off the bus. Annie noticed the signs on the
doors and walls that read:   "Whites Only",
"Colored Drink Here", "No Colored Allowed",
and "Colored Enter Here".   It was then she

learned that all people were not treated the same and that she was a member of a people who were treated badly, and they were called "Colored." She had no desire to ever ride the city bus or leave her community again.

A short time later, Junior, left home to join the Navy. Samantha gave birth to a beautiful baby girl who she named Martha. Jessie and Margaret raised Martha as their own child.

Annie began to notice that the only white people in their neighborhood were Jewish, but although they owned businesses there, they didn't live there.

The "Philip Brush Man" was Mr. Mark, a white person, who came to their home about two or three times a year, selling different canned and bottled products. He dressed in a cheap suit with a dingy white shirt and his oily light brown hair was slicked back on his head. He appeared to ignore the difference in race. When the children saw him coming, they would say, "Here comes the Philip Brush Man."

Mr. Mark always sat out on the front porch and interacted with the kids.

"Here's some candy if you roll your eyes," he offered the kids.

Annie and Claudine would watch as Samantha rolled her eyes. Mr. Mark would then give Samantha two pieces of candy. He gave the other kids only one piece. Sometimes Margaret purchased a small item like a rubbing ornament for pain from him.

When Jessie retired, Mr. Marks stopped coming around. It was years later when Annie learned the significance of the demeaning and racial stereotyped request made by Mr. Marks as it related to the "Eye Rolling".

About two blocks north from Annie's home, on the main street, was a corner grocery store. The store was only a block from the high school. This meant that there was a lot of student traffic in the store. The owner was a Jewish man named Mr. Joe. Annie thought he was a nice person. Margaret had an account with him and she would periodically send the children down to pickup items or to pay on the account.

One day Margaret asked Annie to buy a loaf of bread and to take it to Granny's brother, Uncle Ted (Theodore Fairweather) who lived on the same main street as the store. Annie did as she was told. She walked out of the store and headed down the street towards her great-uncle's house. Annie wasn't aware of a red truck that was following her. Annie saw her uncle sitting outside on his front porch. She climbed up four steps to reach the top of the front yard, walked across the yard, and climbed two more steps to reach the porch.

"Hi, Uncle Ted," Annie greeted him.

"Hey, little one," he said. He stood up and Annie handed him the bread.

"Thanks for bringing this to me. My legs are giving out on me these days, but I do the best I can." Uncle Ted limped as he headed towards his front door.

"Is there anything else I can do for you Uncle Ted?" Annie asked.

"Well, you can come on in and have a little snack with me."

Annie gladly accepted the invitation. Uncle Ted was a widower and had been living alone for several years. He had cooked some corn bread, spinach and chicken. Annie gobbled down all the food on her plate.

"Thank you Uncle Ted, that was so good, I didn't know you could cook like that," she said.

Uncle Ted smiled at the compliment and offered her more. Annie wanted more, but was too embarrassed to accept seconds. Instead, she cleaned off the table and washed the dishes. Annie and Uncle Ted talked a few more minutes before she decided to leave. She told him that she would check in on him every chance she could. That made him happy.

Annie took a shorter route home. She crossed the main street and began to climb a street that had a steep hill. Suddenly, she heard an automobile behind her. There were no sidewalks so she moved over into the grassy area. The vehicle slowed down beside her. She looked back. It was a large red truck driven by a white man who looked to be in his thirties. He raised his lower body up to the window. While still holding the steering wheel and the truck slowly moving, he had his other hand on his erected penis.

"Hey Nigga-gull, you wanna suck on this?" He said to Annie.

Annie gave a quick glance, squealed, and ran through the neighbors' yards. She hid behind a neighbor's house until the truck was no longer in view. Fearful, she then inched towards her home and ran inside. Annie didn't tell anyone. But she did start to develop a fear of White folks.

## CHAPTER 7

### *From Child To Woman*

During that summer, Annie started her menstrual period. Compared to her classmates, she was a late bloomer. Margaret had not talked to Annie about what to do when this happened. But, Annie knew one of her closest friends had already started so she thought she would ask her when she saw her at school. Meanwhile, Annie found some old rags in the closet, folded them and placed them inside her panties to help with the discharge. Annie felt very ill and went to bed.

During the next month's episode, the family could see that something was wrong. Annie vomited all day until there was nothing in her body. She was weak and dehydrated. Margaret gave Annie some aspirins, saltine crackers, and a seven up. This helped hydrate her and ease her pain and discomfort. Margaret, never gave Annie any sanitary pads, so Annie continued to use rags until the next time she got paid from her job. The painful periods occurred every month for several years. Some were so severe that Annie was taken to the military hospital. Needless to say, it was more embarrassing to Annie because everyone knew she was having her period.

One of the doctors had instructed Annie to sit in very warm bath water to ease the pain, but Margaret was against Annie sitting in water during her menstrual.

"Why can't I sit in the tub? The doctor said that the hot water would help my pain?" Annie asked her mother.

"You shouldn't sit in water during that time of month- 'cause that is what my mother told me." Margaret said.

Annie noticed her mother didn't take many baths in the bathtub; instead, she preferred washing from the bathroom sink. One day she got up enough nerves to ask her mother why.

"I'm Methodist; we don't need a lot of water; we sprinkle and don't dip." Margaret told Annie and then laughed.

Annie laughed, but wasn't sure if she wanted to be a Methodist because she loved to dip.

A few times Annie bled through the rags or pads onto the bed sheets. Young Daisy always seemed to have noticed it and would tease Annie by calling her, "Bloody Bloomers". One good thing that came from Annie's experience was that the bedwetting stopped.

**49**

# CHAPTER 8

### Daddy's Home

Although the family remained intact, there were long periods of time when Jessie was absent from home. But, in March, 1963, Jessie returned home. He was officially retired from the USA Army after 27 years of service.

"Is dat my Daddee?" little Aaron asked, when he saw Jessie.

Four year old Aaron, two year old Janis, and one year old Martha did not remember or know Jessie.

Jessie immediately started his job at the VA hospital as a nurse's aide.

Jessie was stationed in North Carolina when his father passed away. He took a leave of absence to attend his father's funeral. Annie remembered her grandfather, Papa Fowler, from visits with her cousins at her Uncle John's house; where Papa Fowler had lived for several years. Jessie looked a lot like him, except his father was taller, thinner and had a darker complexion than he. Like Jessie, Papa Fowler didn't talk much. Although Papa Flower and Granny were divorced, they both attended all of the family gatherings while he lived.

**50**

Jessie tried to adjust to the transition from military life and the reality of taking care of a dozen people in the brutal south; but, it was difficult. Adjusting to the tight living arrangement; his job; and the newly financial needs of the family; created tremendous pressure. Because he had never learned to verbally express himself, he became more physically abusive and began to drink more. To maintain order in the home, Jessie set very strict rules, including curfews. If the children didn't follow them, there were dire consequences.

The master bedroom was in the front of the house next to the front door entrance. Granny's bedroom was in the very rear of the house with her own private entrance. Many times when the older kids went out with their friends and stayed out pass curfew, Granny would let them in through her door no matter what time it was.

Granny, a very large woman, spent most of her time in her room, outside working in the flower garden, or sitting outside in front of her door. Very independent in nature, she cooked all of her meals on a small gas stove that was also used to warm her room during cold seasons. She also had a small refrigerator. Granny's room was attached to the girls' bedroom. Therefore she was required to walk through their room to use the restroom. Because of her 275 pound statue, she needed assistance with crutches or a cane. Consequently, she used a chamber pot for a few days before she carried it to the toilet. On the late nights or early mornings Granny made the trip to the toilet, the stench would wake Annie and she covered her nose from the odor.

Despite such idiosyncratic behavior, all the children loved Granny. Each child would spend a little time with her in her room. Sometimes she would share a piece of her delicious homemade cake patties with the visitor. Annie enjoyed sitting with Granny as she shared many of her family history stories.

Granny's mother was a Native American of the "Black Foot Tribe". Photos of her mother dressed in native garb, alone with her first son, Jessie, and her first grandchild, Elaine, were on her wall. Granny only had one brother, Theodore Fairweather, (Uncle Ted). They were inseparable and always lived in the same community. A large portrait of Granny and Uncle Ted was also on her wall.

Granny never complained about anything, especially about her illnesses. She refused to go to the doctor's office or hospital. She was fearful that she would never return home or worst, she would die. Therefore, she had a doctor that periodically visited her at home.

Jessie's employment with the VA hospital lasted about three years. It became too emotional for him and his experiences with the VA were worse than the entire time he had spent in the military. Jessie felt that the patients were treated inhumanly. There was one highly traumatic experience that triggered his decision to finally leave the VA hospital. A terminal ill patent's screams brought Jessie to his bedside. The patient grabbed Jessie's hand. "I don't want to die." The patient squeezed Jessie's hand so tightly; Jessie thought his hand was broken. In recounting this event, Jessie referred to it as the "Death Hold". Jessie didn't attempt to pull away. Instead he stood there and watched as the patient took his last breath. Finally, Jessie had to pry the deceased patient's gripped hand from his. Jessie resigned shortly after that incident.

# Chapter 9

## *Cruelty*

Although Jessie only finished the tenth grade, he read all the time; at least two newspapers. One newspaper was thick, had a lot of white people in it, coupons, cartoons, and an abundance of information. The other newspaper was thin, had pictures of Colored people in it, and not a lot of information. Annie learned that one was written by Colored people and the other was written by White people. When her father was done, she would ask permission to see the papers. When Annie first started reading the paper, it was only to see the cartoons and ads. Annie loved to read "Little Orphan Annie". Although, she was named after one of her mother's sisters, Annie's relatives would tease her by claiming she was named after "Little Orphan Annie" because Annie was born with a reddish afro.

One day Annie saw her father sitting in his chair with the newspaper in his hands. But, rather than resting contentedly, this time he was gripping it and there was so much sadness in his face. He was holding the Colored people newspaper. She waited until he was finished.

Again, she asked permission to see the paper. This time Annie went straight to the

**54**

Colored newspaper. Right there on the front page of the paper was a photo of three people hanging from a tree. There were pictures of white people standing around smiling and some just staring. Annie noticed that the people hanging from the tree were all colored. There were one young girl and two young boys who all seemed to be around Annie's age.

Annie had always felt safe with her father being home, but suddenly she felt scared and lost. She turned the page and saw a photo of a burning cross in front of someone's house. Standing beside it, she saw a person wearing a white hood and robe.

"How anyone could be so brutal and hateful?" Annie thought.

Annie began to see the world very differently. She could not understand how the so called White Christians truly believed that they were better than everyone else in the world. This was a rude awakening for Annie. She felt less safe than ever and feared white people even more. But, for the presence of her father, Annie's trauma would have been much greater; for Jessie constantly sought to keep this family safe.

Each night before Jessie went to bed, he would check the doors and windows and he turned off all gas items. There was a gas floor heater in the front living room and a heater in the girl's room. Granny had a heater in her room. Jessie claimed he turned the gas off for safety and to cut down on the cost of the utilities. Margaret would usually get up early before the kids awake and turn on the heat so that the house wouldn't be too cold.

On this particular morning, November 23, 1963, Margaret had slept in a little longer. When Annie woke up to get ready for school, the house was freezing. It was a Friday and Annie had to take an exam in math. Annie jumped up grabbed her clothes and ran into Granny's room. Granny was an early riser. Annie could smell bacon cooking so she knew Granny's room would be warm. Annie got fully dressed and went into the bath to brush her teeth and comb her hair. Granny offered Annie a piece of bacon and a biscuit. Annie had a difficult time eating early in the morning, but decided to accept the sandwich to take to school. Granny wrapped it in a piece of wax paper and handed it to Annie. Annie thanked Granny and went out the back door to head for school.

When Annie stepped out into the weather, it was a cold morning and the winds were very strong. She dressed warmly in a long coat with a sweater and a wool skirt. Girls weren't allowed to wear pants in schools at that time; she wore long wool socks, and a pair of loafers. Annie watched children running after their hats, scarves and school bags that had been blown away by the wind. Annie had difficulty keeping her skirt down; and could feel the cold breeze on her legs and on her face. Annie tied her scarf firmly on her head so that her hair didn't get too ruffled from the wind. She walked swiftly against the heavy winds and waved or yelled hello to the children who passed her.

Finally, she reached the school and went to her homeroom class, where her teacher, Ms. Walker, was talking with a few students. The school felt nice and warm so Annie took off her coat and hung it in her locker.

The day went very well for Annie. She completed her math exam and felt that she had done very well. Annie's last class period was chemistry. She entered the classroom, but the teacher was standing outside talking with other teachers. She sat down at her desk and took out her book to wait on the teacher. Annie heard one of the teachers crying. She and the other students wondered what was going on. A few minutes later, the teacher came in and he announced to the students, "President John F. Kennedy has been assassinated."

The students became very emotional, some cried, and a couple of students ran out of the classroom.

Annie wasn't able to share her true emotions in public, yet she felt tormented and frightened. Annie truly loved JFK, especially Jackie. She had kept up with everything about them. Again, she didn't understand why someone would kill another person simply because he thought all people were equal.

But later, Annie had another experience that taught her lessons about violence.

Although a relative newcomer in her neighborhood, it had not been difficult for Annie to fit into the lives of the other teens. She thought everyone was so nice and she felt free to walk down any streets, without any problems, in the neighborhood with her siblings and friends. Everyone would greet each other and some would stop and have friendly conversations. What Annie wasn't prepared for or even aware of was that a neighbor on the street directly behind her house was territorial and didn't care for her.

The neighborhood high school included students in seventh through twelfth grades. Annie was 13 years old and in the seventh grade. It was her first year and she had joined the school's band and majorettes. About half way through the school year, Annie was confronted by

a girl, named Niki, who was in the eighth grade.
She lived on the street behind Annie's house.
Annie was familiar with Niki and her family.
Niki's younger brother was the same age as Annie
and she had a younger sister. Niki was much
taller than Annie. She was thin with nice dark
hair, dark skin, and a pretty face. Annie didn't
understand why Niki was so upset with her. One
day Annie was walking down the street.

"I'm going to kick your butt." Niki
shouted.

Annie, confused, walked away and headed
home. Yes, the threats continued and Annie
would take different routes home to avoid Niki.
Finally, one day Annie became tired of running.
Niki, again with a couple of her friends in
tow, followed Annie down the street to Annie's
home.

"You think you're cute. Red Bitch! You
ain't Shit. I will kick your ass." Niki shouted
at Annie.

A couple of neighbors had come out
of their homes. Fearful, Annie didn't look back
and said nothing. She kept walking until she
felt hands that shoved her with great force.
Annie quickly turned around. Everything began
to happen in slow motion as if it were a movie
or a dream.  She heard screams. When Annie

regained her awareness, she heard her brother, Robert Lee, voice.

"Annie let her neck go - let it go." Annie realized that she was on top of Niki with her hands on her neck.

"Annie let go of Niki's neck, "Girrrrl", you were screaming so loud we thought she was killing you," Robert Lee said.

Annie realized that it was her own screams that she had heard. Robert Lee helped Annie on to her feet. Niki's friends helped her on her feet and they walked away towards her house. When Annie became totally aware of what had happened, she felt relieved.

"If you want some more, you know where to find me," Annie shouted to Niki.

Annie was tired of living in fear. That day, Annie made a statement and never had to fight again.

# CHAPTER 10

*Raising A Family*

Margaret was raised in a Christian Methodist Episcopal home and was accustomed to going to church on a regular basis. While traveling during the military life, Margaret always looked for a church for the family.

In contrast, Jessie did not go to church, unless it was a funeral or a wedding. He was a spiritual man, but didn't see the need for weekly worship. Sometimes friends or relatives invited Jessie to join them at church for communion.

"I had communion last night," he replied, referring to the white lightning he had drunk.

Jessie and Margaret had zero tolerance for disruptive and disrespectful children. They insisted that their children behave in public, and respect adults and the law. They loved taking their children on trips and visiting relatives and friends. The children sat down, spoke when they were spoken to, and responded with, "Yes Ma'am, Yes Sir." They were often referred to as "Little Solders". Many people complimented Jessie and Margaret on how proper and well behaved their children were.

The family had scheduled meals, especially breakfast and dinner. If the child had not eaten by 7:30 a.m., then usually everything was gone or put away. But dinner was much different. It was everyday at 5:00 p.m. If a child wasn't there, they simply did not eat.

Every Sunday, Margaret woke up the children to get them ready for church. She combed their hair and made breakfast. Margaret dressed, "The Twins", Claudine and Annie, in similar or identical outfits. In most cases, the only difference would be the color.

When Margaret and the children returned from church, the children would scatter to change clothes. Sunday's dinner had always been cooked on Saturday evening. Margaret went to the kitchen to get the prepared food from the refrigerator. A couple of the girls would help her prepare for dinner.

Margaret loved a formal table setting. She never used paper plates. The table had a beautiful table cloth. It was set with china, water glasses, and silverware. Once the table was set, Jessie took his place at the head of the table. Margaret was always the last person to sit down. She sat nearest the kitchen door and next to Jessie. He said his usual grace before each meal.

"Lord, make us truly thankful for the food we are about to receive and for the nourishment of our bodies; For Christ sakes."

"Amen", everyone said.

"Lord, bless the cook and have mercy on the dish washer," someone else would say.

Jessie was a very fast eater. Annie was a lot like him; but a light eater. Margaret was just the opposite, she ate extremely slowly. That day the menu consisted of turnip greens, potato salad, cornbread, sliced cucumbers, onions and tomatoes, chitterlings, and bread pudding. While the family talked about some funny things that had happened, Annie slid her chitterlings to another family member. She hated chitter-lings. Margaret caught her and put another small piece on her plate.

"Now eat it", Margaret demanded.

Annie stuffed her mouth with so much cornbread she barely had room in her mouth for anything else- but she managed to stick the piece of meat in also. She continued to chew until she swallowed. She prayed her mother would not give her another piece. She didn't.

The family dinners were filled with laughter. Jessie was not a talker, but sometimes he would smile. When Margaret told a funny story, she would laugh so hard that she had to hold her stomach and out came a loud fart. Everybody at the table knew the source of that noise. But Margaret, with a serious face, pushed the table cloth forward at her lap height, looked under the table.

"Scat cat, was that you? - git out of here," Margret would say.

Everyone laughed and slowly moved from the table. Margaret was always the last person to leave the table.

Since there was no electrical dishwasher, Annie was usually the dishwasher that for which the prayer was asking mercy for. The others would help clear the table and put away the food, but the dishes were left for Annie.

"When I get my own home, I will never have a formal dining room," Annie swore. But she loved and appreciated the family time together.

# CHAPTER 11

## *Country Folks*

During the 1950's and 60's large families were the norm, but folks who lived in the "country" sometimes had even larger families. One favorite activity of Annie's family was gathering the children in a station wagon and taking a trip to the country to visit aunts, uncles and cousins. Margaret's oldest sister, Mary, had ten children; they lived in a house about the same size as Margaret's, but without an indoor bathroom. During one of these visits, Annie had to use the bathroom. She tried to hold it as long as she could because she knew she would have to face the mean rooster who lived near the outhouse and freely controlled the yard. For some reason, Annie never understood why mean dogs, horses and roosters gravitated towards her; she had been bitten and pecked by them. Annie held her bodily fluids as long as she could. Finally, she asked her mother if she could use the bathroom. One of the young cousins walked with Annie to the outhouse toilet. About three feet from the door to the small building, the rooster charged at Annie. Annie screamed and ran. She reached the door just before the rooster could peck her. After using the toilet, she noticed there was no toilet paper. Unsure what to do, she simply sat there for a while praying that someone would come looking for her. No one came. After a while longer, she noticed that the residual body fluid had dried itself during the wait. Still uncomfortable and feeling sorted, she slowly cracked open the wooden door and looked around. No one was in sight, not even the rooster. Annie took off running towards the door to the house. When she entered, everyone was eating. She quickly poured water into a "wash pan" and went into another room to wash her body and her hands. She couldn't wait to share the meal that had been prepared. Annie was a picky eater, but she loved desserts. She saw the cooked chicken, but that only made her think about the mean ole rooster. Her recent experience only allowed her to eat some greens and a piece of pound cake.

Annie urged her parents to leave shortly after the meal. She didn't want another experience with the mean ole rooster. In addition, she wanted to get home in time to watch Roy Rogers and Dale Evans.

There was only one television and one telephone in the Fowler's home. The TV was in the living room and the telephone was in the corner of the dining room. Granny didn't have either in her room. The family did not watch a lot of television together because the children were busy with outside activities. Jessie enjoyed watching sports, documentaries and the news channels. Margaret liked soap operas such "As the World Turns", and "Guiding Light". She also enjoyed listening to gospel and country music on the radio. One of her favorite country stars was Tennessee Ernie Ford; she always tuned in to his weekly show.

While living in Germany, the family didn't watch much TV. This was because the USA TV shows were limited to the "Arthur Godfrey Time" (both on TV and radio), and western movies. Once back in the states, the family watched a few TV shows together. Two of the children's favorite shows were the "Little Rascals" and "Amos and Andy". The children got so excited when they saw a Colored person on a TV show or in a movie.

"Yall hurry up, come and see, there's a Colored person on TV," Someone would yell out. Everyone would run to the TV and give praises.

Every year, the family watched seasonal repeated movies like, "Gone With The Wind", "The Wonderful Wizard of Oz", "I Passed For White", "Carmen Jones" and "Porgy and Bess". Other TV shows that the family enjoyed were, "Father Knows Best" and "I love Lucy".

Annie loved western movies and television shows. In addition to "Roy Rogers and Dale Evans", she was a fan of "Lone Rangers" and the "Rifle Man". During those times the movies and

TV shows portrayed the cowboys as the good guys and they wore white hats. The Native Americans (then called Indians), were depicted as the bad guys. As a pre-teen, Annie had a re-occurring nightmare: (*She dreamt that her mother told her that she could no longer live with the family. Her mother had made Annie pack up everything. They arrived at a house where an Indian woman, fully dressed in native clothing, came to the door. Her mother pushed Annie towards the woman. The woman reached for Annie and said, "I will take care of you."*) Annie always woke up screaming, "No, No".

When Annie was a teen, she was a true fan of David Janssen who starred in the TV show "The Fugitive". She didn't think of him as handsome or sexy, but was drawn to his character that people misunderstood and treated unfairly. She also watched the "Sonny & Cher" show and tried to emulate Cher's body type and fashion styles. Annie worked out hard to keep her tummy flat and firm. She also made similar fun outfits like Cher's. As a result, even at 64 years of age, Annie's firm and slender tight body allowed her to wear similar fashions.

# CHAPTER 12

## Discipline

In the 21st century parents can go to jail for physically punishing their children. This was not the case when Annie was a child and teen. Jessie and Margaret believed in punishing their children by taking away privileges and giving whippings. The children dreaded both, but really tried to avoid the whippings. Jessie would hit with anything nearby or with his hands. Margaret had inherited her thick bones and large hands from her father and they were pretty powerful when she hit. Every child had felt her hands one way or another. If one didn't move fast enough or said something inappropriate, then "The hand" would be felt across the butt or anywhere she could reach. But, there were other times when Margaret would take her time in doling out punishment to her children. Specifically, she would first demand that he or she go outside and break a switch from the tall hedges grown along the property line. The first time Annie had to get the switch; she found the smallest switch, took off the leaves, and handed it to her mother. Margaret sent her back outside to get another. The switch was still too small. Annie then had to go into the yard and harvest a third switch. Margaret then

**69**

twisted the switches together and spanked Annie's legs. The punishment was so severe, but it taught Annie to adhere to her parent's rules. As a result, she didn't have to get any more switches, but she occasionally got the "Big Hand". Just the threat of the hand,

"I will knock you out," Margaret sometimes said, was enough to correct any disapproving action.

Another example of Jessie's discipline was when he told a child to complete a chore and the child didn't do it; when the family lived in Missouri, Jessie took the family to several baseball games to watch Junior and Robert Lee play. On one of Robert Lee's game days, Jessie gave him instructions to complete a chore before he went to the game. At this particular game, Robert Lee was the next batter up. Out of nowhere, Jessie went onto the field and grabbed Robert Lee by his shirt collar. Jessie pulled him off the field and he commenced to whipping Robert Lee until another parent intervened.

"This is none of your business, so it's best you back away," Jessie told the man.

The man did just that.

"You should have finished your chores before you came to this game," Jessie explained to Robert Lee.

Needless to say, Robert Lee did not finish that game, and he returned home to complete his chores.

As quickly as Jessie is to discipline his children, he is just as quick to defend them-- when they were in the right.

The Jones family lived on the east side of Jessie's house and included three boys and one girl. Each of the four Jones kids was the same ages as four of Jessie's children. The kids played together and visited each other.

The Jones' had a tall pecan tree in their backyard. A few of the large branches on the tree hung over onto Jessie's property. During the fall, some of the pecans and abundance of leaves fell into Jessie's yard.

One day Junior ran into the house and told Jessie about an altercation.

"Daddy, Mr. Jones hit me." Junior told his father.

"Why? Jessie asked.

"Because- I picked up some pecans."

"Were you on their property?"

"No Sir, I was in our backyard and I put them in my pocket," Junior explained.

Jessie walked Junior over to the Jones' house and knocked on their door. Mr. Jones came to the door.

"Yeah!" he said to Jessie.

"Did you hit my son?"

**71**

"Yeah I did. Those are my pecans, not yours."

"Those are your damn leaves too. And don't you ever put your hands on any of my children again. The next time you come on my property, it better be to pick up the damn leaves," Jessie shouted.

Mr. Jones never came on the property again. But, not too long after that, Annie was outside picking up pecans in the back yard when she heard a woman scream from the other side of the hedges that divided the properties. It was Mrs. Jones looking over the hedges at Annie.

"Gull, don't you touch them pecans. Those ain't yours," she said.

"These ain't our damn leaves either, so you can come git them too," Annie said, without a thought.

Like father -Like daughter.

# CHAPTER 13

## *Critters*

The family home was built in the early forties and was not well insulated. This caused the house to become infested with rats and roaches. Indeed, Annie could not recall when there weren't any pests in the home. Sometimes rats would walk across the beds while the children were sleeping or walk right in front of the TV while the family was looking at it. They were some gutsy critters. When a person turned on the light in the kitchen, dozens of roaches would scatter to get away. But, sometimes the family could be sitting down for a meal and a few roaches would crawl along the wall. These circumstances created a few embarrassing moments when company was present.

Jessie, who was always a "do it yourself" kind of person, made an effort to keep the critters out of the house. He would place rat traps and bait everywhere. The problem with that was it was difficult to find the dead rats that died from eating the bait. This meant that the house would smell awful for a few days after a rat had died.

As far as the roaches, Jessie would put together a liquid concoction. He forewarned the family that he would be spraying the house for roaches. During those times, the family left the house for several hours. Jessie would tightly shut the house and spray. After the waiting period, the family would come back. The odor in the house was still unbearable, even after windows were opened and the fans were running. A few days later, a few roaches would show up again. The family laughed and agreed that the only thing Jessie's concoction was good for was to get rid of the "two legged critters."

In some instances, Jessie was required to protect his family from "two-legged critters". The windows in the rear bedrooms were low in the family home. Since there wasn't any central a/c, oftentimes the windows were left open. The girls loved the fresh, spring breeze while they slept in two full beds. One bed was pushed against the east window, where Annie and Claudine slept, and the other against the west wall, where Daisy, Janis and Martha slept. The space between the beds allowed a walkway from Granny's room to the bathroom.

One night, a prowler ripped the screen from the window and crawled through it and got on top of Claudine. Annie was asleep beside her sister, Claudine. But, she was awakened by her sister's screams. The man ran back through the window when Claudine screamed. Fortunately, no one was hurt. The police were called, Claudine gave them a description, but there wasn't much more they could do. The incident weighed heavily on Jessie. He locked every door and window that night and within a few days, he had bars on every window throughout the house. Jessie also purchased a yard dog.

# Chapter 14

*City Boy Turned Country*

On many occasions, Margaret told her children about how happy she had been to get out of the country when she got married to a city boy. She never thought her city boy husband would turn country on her.

Jessie, despite his occasional friendship with alcohol and his strict child rearing practices, was a good husband and father. Jessie did whatever was needed to care for his large family. Hard work did not bother him. Moreover, he taught his hard work ethics to his children. When Jessie retired from the military, he knew he would need supplemental income to feed his children. He was a proud man and refused to accept welfare. Thus, he would budget his income very carefully to insure that all of his family needs were met.

In the contrast, Margaret was very different than Jessie regarding her spending habits. She never grasped the concept of financial planning or saving. If she were given $10, she would immediately spend $10. She would open credit accounts without worrying about how it would be paid back. On the other hand, Jessie based how he would spend the $10 by thinking on a long-term basis. He would save

$2 and stretch the $8 through barter and trade. Margaret was willing to accept charity and government supplements, but would not let Jessie know about it.

One strategy Jessie used to obtain fresh produce for his family was unique. Jessie had relatives that were share croppers. He made arrangements to go out to their properties during harvesting time to pick vegetables. After his relatives had picked what they wanted, Jessie would take his family out to pick what was left. Sometimes there were beans, peas, potatoes, melons, tomatoes, greens, or okra. Anything that was offered, Jessie accepted. After harvesting, the family returned home and prepared the food for freezing and pickling. One time Jessie took his movie camera to the field when the family was harvesting. The family wore straw hats and outfits, and made dance moves that emulated the TV show called, "Hee Haw". The family always tried to convert hard times into fun times.

Jessie didn't stop at harvesting, for it was only one mean of feeding his family. Jessie went hunting with his buddies and relatives. He bought bulk meats with other families by sharing the cost. Jessie brought home fresh games such as: rabbit; deer; calf; goat; beef; and pork.

Jessie bought a large used freezer to store the meat. It had a lock on it and was placed outside in the unattached garage. Once, he brought home about seventy pounds of freshly slaughtered beef for the family, and put it in the freezer. Annie could see the pride on Jessie's face. Needless to say, the family looked forward to the "good eats.

About a month later, Annie heard her father shout out one of his phrases when he was really upset,

"Good Gracious Alive!"

Annie and a few other family members ran outside to see what had happened. Jessie was standing over the freezer pulling meat out of it. The smell was awful. None of the meat could be saved; the freezer was broken. Annie could see the sadness on her father's face and felt so bad for him.

One day he brought home a possum. As usual, he threw it on the table for country girl, Margaret, to clean and cook. Margaret took one look at the possum and told Jessie;

"You better get that big rat off my table and out of this house."

Jessie did just that. The family never ate possum.

Jessie also loved the outdoors and found the time to take his family fishing along the nearby lakes and the Mississippi River. Jessie didn't throw back any of the fish, no matter what size. Annie learned at an early age how to clean and cook fish. She looked forward to the outings because being near the water always reminded her of the time the family cruised down the Rhine River in Europe.

Although Jessie wasn't a church going man, he was kind-hearted and didn't mind sharing food with the neighbors and relatives. For example, he would set aside produce and deliver it in person.

One day during the summer school break, Jessie came home in a chicken truck. He was riding with his cousin who had a chicken farm. Jessie had bought twenty hens and brought them home. The children's excitement about the chickens lasted only a moment for they quickly learned the chickens would eventually be slaughtered and that they had been chosen as the assassins.

Nevertheless, the "chicken affair" became a family affair. Jessie placed three large crates of chickens in the back yard near the back door. Early the next morning when the children woke up, Margaret had already begun bowling large pots of water. Granny was sitting outside in her chair next to her bedroom entrance. Beside her was a very large metal washtub. After the children ate a quick breakfast, Jessie told the boys to go with him outside. Margaret and Samantha took the bowling water out and poured it into the washtub.

Annie stood inside looking through the screen door as the family prepared for the slaughter. She became a bit nervous when she saw Jessie with a large ax and talking to her brothers. Jessie took one of the chickens out of the crate by its neck. He gave it several jerks in a quick circular motion. He then raised his ax and chopped off the chicken's head. The chicken's lower part kept jerking and moving for a moment longer. One of the chickens was on the ground running with its head chopped off. Annie thought she would pass out. She covered her eyes just as Margaret told her to move out the way. Margaret, carrying a large bowl, rags, newspapers, and paper bags in her hands, rushed outside. A few minutes later, Margaret called the girls to her side for a "show n' tell" of what needed to be done. Margaret and Granny demonstrated the process of cleaning the chickens. They dunked the dead hens into the hot water and let them stay for a moment.

"Ugh-h-h," the girls said as they held their noses from the fresh kill smell.

Then Margaret took one chicken and Granny took another. They quickly pulled the feathers out of the chicken. Once the feathers were removed, Margaret took a knife and cut a larger hole around the hen's butt. She passed the knife to Granny to do the same. Margaret then inserted one hand into the hole and she pulled out the guts. The girls panicked and swore that they just couldn't do it.

"You better get busy!" Margaret fussed and demanded.

The washtub had about six hens in it. Samantha, Claudine and Annie each pulled a hen from the tub and placed it on some news- paper. The girls continued to pluck the hens' feathers, but none cut the butt. Margaret decided to let the girls pluck and wash the chickens while she and Granny cut and gutted the hens. Annie tried hard to be strong and not disappoint her parents. She took a few hens to the sink to wash them. Annie had washed store-bought chickens before; therefore, she felt comfortable with the task; until she reached in a couple of times and found more guts, bowel, and eggs. Annie continued until the task was finished. However, she was unable to eat any of the freshly killed hens.

Jessie had tremendous respect for the farmers' hard work and he greatly admired his father-in-law who had also raised eleven children on what was grown and raised. Jessie also felt he'd been greatly blessed by marrying one of his father-in-law's beautiful children. In buying those twenty hens, Jessie was paying homage to the man who fathered and raised a woman whom he dearly loved.

Finally, all hens were killed, cleaned, and placed in the freezer. Two hens were cooked for dinner. At long last the family relaxed. Margaret had a way of making a bad day end in a good day. She had the children select and play some 45 records. It didn't matter what song was played; once the music started, Margaret got on the floor and showed off her own style of the Lindy hop, foxtrot, and apple jack. Jessie sat back and enjoyed the view.

Annie and a couple other siblings would join Margaret, doing their own freestyle of dancing.

"Go white girl, go white girl," Samantha called out to mock Annie's dance style.

Annie didn't have the soulful style of dancing as her siblings; but it was all in fun for Annie. She kept on dancing.

Everyone laughed and forgot about the difficult day.

# CHAPTER 15

### Tomboy

Annie's greatest escape was going to school. She joined every school activity she could to keep her mind off of the family issues and the racial society outside her community. She joined the marching and concert bands, the drama club, and was a majorette.

Annie's two favorite teachers were her math and drama teachers. She loved how they took the time to explain each step. But, Annie did not take the time she should to study. She felt dumb because she had a difficult time concentrating or focusing on any homework. There was very little privacy or space to study at home. When she arrived home there were always chores and sometimes disagreements arose between her parents or siblings. Annie sometimes participated in school activities to avoid going home.

Annie was and had always been a tom-boy. As a part of her "tom boyishness", Annie agreed to play on the girl's flag football team at the high school. It was a new sport and the school was testing it out. Annie played center and captain for the offense and outside-linebacker for the defense. She was pretty good

**83**

at it. After a few weeks of practices, the school announced the first game. On that evening, students, parents, friends and relatives gathered at the high school's football stadium. It was the first time girl's flag-football game was played. It consisted of two halves of 15 minutes each.

Annie started her period on the day of the game. She was in great discomfort from the cramps and her head ached as if it was going to split open.  To better cope, she took a couple of aspirins and was determined to play. Annie looked out into the crowd for her family members and friends. As the captain, she and the other team captain walked up to the referee who flipped the coin.

Annie's offense team received the ball. Everyone got into position. The game began. Annie passed the ball to the quarterback.  The quarterback passed it to the running back (Annie's best friend, Leola). Leola ran far and fast, but the defense grabbed her flag.

The game went pretty well up to the last few minutes of the first half.  There was no score on the board.  Leola had taken the ball 18 yards from the gold line, Annie, still in pain, passed the ball to the quarterback. The defense came fast and hard towards the offense. Annie was tackled so hard she was knocked to the ground. She felt as if her head had fallen from her body. The referee gave penalties to the defense.

Annie got up and passed the ball again. This time when the defense came, Annie's team was ready to tackle back. There were more penalties given on both sides. This process continued throughout the game. Finally, about half way through the second half, the referee threw in the flag and called it a tie. The crowd seemed to have enjoyed it, but, needless to say, there was no longer a "girl's flag football" team. To Annie, it was all good.

# CHAPTER 16

## *In charge*

The personal freedom that had allowed Annie to be a leader in activities at school ended. Now, at 16 years old, her five older siblings had left home. Elaine and Claudine lived in Oregon, Junior and Robert Lee had joined the Navy, and Samantha moved into her own place not too far away. Trying to retain decent grades, work a part-time job, continue with band and drama, complete far more home chores, and intermediate disputes, Annie felt overwhelmed.

Annie was very sensitive and observant about crises that occurred in the family. She felt that she should be able to help solve them.

Because Margaret was active in the church choir and PTA, Annie had even more responsibilities. Moreover, these became enlarged when Margaret dealt with health issues and sometimes checked herself into the hospital for a few days at a time. Annie took full responsibility for her younger five siblings. Sometimes, arguments would occur and Annie was required to create peace.

On one occasion, Annie reprimanded her brother, Donny, so badly about something quite minor. He reacted by putting his fist through the wall; instead of hitting her. Annie felt badly that she caused her brother to react in such a way. She knew that both, he and she, would probably get a beaten for the damage. And so, she had to devise a plan.

Annie was an observant and curious person. She always watched her father while he was doing repair work around the house and yard. Annie grabbed some newspaper and used some to stuff the hole in the wall. She then found some plaster that was in the outside tool shed. She added water to make a thick paste. She then filled the hole until it was full and even. When it dried, she used sandpaper to smooth it. Annie could not find a matching paint, but placed a photo on top of the repaired wall. Her father never noticed the damage.

As the oldest sibling at home, she was also required to use her "handyman" skills at other times. One summer night, it was about eighty degrees inside of the house. This made it impossible for Annie to sleep. The portable fan was broken because a rat or some critter had bitten through the fan's cord. Annie went to the outside tool shed and found some electrical tape. She also found a razor blade in the bathroom. Annie cut the fan wires with the blade and reattached the wires with the electrical tape. It worked.

Other duties Annie felt she had been empowered to do, were to keep the younger siblings groomed. She washed and hung the clothes and combined the hair of her younger sisters. The first time Annie tried barbering was with her brother Donny. After she left a couple of large bald spots on his head, he never allowed her to touch his head again. But cute little Aaron was an excellent model for Annie. He had the biggest head for a child; he was nick named "Headquarters" or "Head" for short. Aaron was so easy going.

Annie placed a chair near an outlet. When Aaron sat down, Annie covered him with a towel and plugged in her father's electric clippers. Aaron never moved even when Annie said, "Whoops," which meant she got to close to his scalp. When Annie finished, Aaron got up and never said a word -even with the half dozen bald spots on his head. Thanks to Aaron, after a little more practice, Annie got much better with the clippers.

One day, Annie came home, but couldn't get into the front door. She went to the back door and entered through the kitchen. She saw her father working. He had knocked out the wall that separated the living room and dining room.

It had turned into a large open, single space with a wide arch in the center. It had been painted and now Jessie was putting in hardwood floors. Annie could hardly do her own chores, she was so fascinated by watching Jessie work.

The next day when Annie arrived home, she still couldn't get through the front door. When she did enter from the kitchen, she saw two rooms that were beautiful. Jessie had completed the rooms, but the floors were still wet with stain and varnish. It would be another day before the family would be able to walk on it.

Annie and her younger siblings felt so proud of the work their father had done. They invited their relatives and friends to see their new space. Some thought they were rich; but, Annie knew then that they were not rich. She fully understood that achievements in life occurred through hard work.

# CHAPTER 17

### *Caught In the Middle*

In some respects, Annie, the middle child felt caught in the middle. On one cold winter and very challenging day, Annie came home from one of her jobs, hungry and tired. The sink was stacked with dirty dishes. When Annie looked in the bedroom that she shared with her sisters, she saw her maternal grandmother lying down on her bed. Annie thought she was sleep, so she quickly turned and quietly left the room. The bathroom door was locked, so she rushed to the kitchen sink to wash her hands and opened the refrigerator to find something to eat. Margaret stepped out of the bathroom.

"Hi Annie, when you change your clothes, wash the dishes.

"Hi, yes Ma'am."

"Then you need to stay home to watch the children, and help them with their homework. I have to go out."

"If you can't take care of your own children, why do you keep having them?" Annie blurted out to her mother as she threw dirty pans into the sink.

As soon as the words escaped her mouth echoing those stored-up thoughts, Annie knew she was going to get a beating; she shrugged her shoulders and thought "I don't care." She was too tired, hungry and burned out to care. Margaret just stared at Annie.

"Beat her! Spit on her! Slap her!" Margaret's mother shouted, whose mouth stood open based on the audacity of Annie's remarks.

Margaret gave Annie another stare and simply walked away.

For a while Annie wondered how she escaped a beaten for that disrespectful comment she made to her mother. But, several years later Margaret brought up the incident to Annie, who had forgotten about it. Margaret explained to Annie that the comment she made to her was disrespectful, but it was a true statement. Although long overdue, Annie apologized to her mother.

The following Friday evening, Annie came home after visiting one of her friends. When she entered the house, she heard her mother screaming. She ran to the back of the house and entered the girl's bedroom. There she saw her father punching her mother who was pinned against the wall. Annie pleading to her father to let her mother, jumped between them.

"Stop Daddy, let her go!"

Jessie, drunk and stumbling, was distracted by Annie's screams and allowed Margaret to free herself. Annie was still standing next to Jessie when she made more attempts to distract Jessie as Margaret ran out the door and down the drive way. Jessie grabbed Annie and began punching her. Annie was in shock.

"Daddy, stop! Stop, Daddy! I'm sorry, I'm sorry!"

Jessie stopped and walked towards another room of the house. Annie ran from the house to find her mother. She found her mother at a neighbor's house. Annie asked her mother if she was okay. Margaret rubbed the bruises on her arm and said, "Yes, I'm okay."

Annie was still in shock. Jessie had never hit Annie before. Annie knew he had beaten her mother and a few of her siblings; but not her. Annie had received several beatings from her mother, but never from her father. Confused, Annie sat down in the neighbor's house with her mother. Annie's mother never asked her how she was doing or what had happened to her. Annie looked down at her feet and noticed that she had only one shoe on. Annie had bought the shoes about a week before. The other shoe was never found.

The safety Annie felt at home was never the same. She didn't feel safe anywhere. Annie asked herself:

"Who will protect me?

"How will I ever feel safe?"

# CHAPTER 18

*Hungry*

Annie began working as a bus girl at a top local restaurant during her junior year in high school. Colored people were not allowed to patron the restaurant, nor could they be a waitress. They could only clean and cook. Annie's sister, Samantha, worked there once as a cook, and Margaret sewed and tailored for one of the waitresses named, Monica. Annie would never forget her experience there, because she received a second degree burn on her inner armed that left a life-time scar. Annie worked there for about a year at three nights a week from 4pm to midnight. She traveled by bus from school and back home. The restaurant owners did not give meals to their workers, but offered a small discount. With the discount, Annie thought it still cost too much.

Sometimes Annie would stop by the neighborhood grocery store and buy a .05 cents pack of crackers, .15 cents worth of bologna, a dill or sour pickle for .03 cents, and four cookies for .02 cents; all for a quarter. Annie would try to eat something before she went to work. But, there were times when she didn't have the opportunity to eat at all.

After leaving the restaurant, Annie arrived home about one o'clock in the morning or later. Sometimes she would have homework assignments to complete, but not until she washed the dirty dishes left for her. There was never a food plate set aside for her; nor was any food left. To fight the occasional hunger, Annie heated up the "pot liquor" that was left from the greens or whatever had been cooked. She found a piece of cornbread or crackers and crumbled it in the liquid. Annie felt very frustrated and felt as if no one cared about her and that there wasn't enough support for her. Annie never complained; she seemed physically fit and normal to others around her. But inside, she felt tormented and she didn't know how much more she had to give. Annie cried in silence.

There were times when Annie did not get to bed until about three o'clock in the morning and had not completed her assignments. She still had to get up at 6:30 a.m. to arrive on time for her first class at 8 a.m. Annie often skipped breakfast and forgot to take her lunch. When she did arrive at school, she could barely keep her eyes open and concentrate on the lectures. When lunch time came she was too proud to ask her classmates to share their food. But, when they offered her food, Annie gladly accepted. She devoured the food from

hunger and she sometimes was teased for eating
the food so fast.

# CHAPTER 19

*First Kiss*

Annie loved her high school. It was only a few blocks from the house. But, on cold and icy days, it seemed to take much longer to get there.

During her high school years, Annie was very friendly and outgoing. She loved to talk to everyone. She didn't care about being with the popular girls or being popular. Annie truly did not know how beautiful she was on the outside, as well as, on the inside. By the age of 16, Annie had grown to be five feet seven inches. She was a bit flat chest; her breast barely filled a size A cup. She had a small waist and a flat tummy. She had a small butt, and her legs were athletic with thick calves. Annie inherited her fair skin complexion and freckles from her mother and her kinky thick hair from her father. She wore her hair below her shoulders, and it was a natural sandy auburn brown color. She was also blessed to have her father's large brown eyes.

The boys at her school seemed very immature to Annie. The so-called "pretty boys" were a turn off to Annie because they reminded her of her older brothers whose behavior weren't too impressive to her. See didn't think

**97**

that the boys at school or her brothers were "All That". She was unaware of the secret admirers she had. There was one of them who eventually made it known to her that he liked her. Thomas was a guitar and trumpet player in the school's concert band. He also played center and was the captain of the football team.  Annie played the flute in the concert band and was a majorette during the football season.  Therefore, Thomas and Annie would see each other at rehearsals. Thomas was very polite and told funny stories. Annie liked Thomas, but didn't feel any sparks for him. She thought of him as a very good friend.

On her 16th birthday, after band practice, and in the school hall way, Thomas handed Annie a small box that was gift wrapped with red ribbons. Annie stared at the box. She had never received a gift from anyone other than her immediate family. She opened the box and continues to stare at the beautiful gold ring.

"Happy Birthday Annie, hope you like it," Thomas said.

The ring sat in the center of the box and had a small amethyst stone and a single pearl mounted on it. Annie smiled.

"This is so beautiful, Thomas. Thank you. You shouldn't have done this."

"I would do anything for you- will you be my girl?" Thomas asked.

Annie was shocked, but quick to respond.

"Thomas I can't date you and my parents won't allow me to date anyone. I like you like a friend."

"Well, that's good, so as a friend can I come visit you at your house?" Thomas asked.

"Yes, I guess so," Annie said.

A few weeks later on a beautiful spring day, Thomas walked Annie home from school. She introduced him to her parents. Jessie wasn't too happy about Annie bringing any boys around, but he'd rather she did that instead of sneaking out to see them.

Annie and Thomas filled a couple of glasses with water and went into the backyard. They sat on a little bench that was in front of Granny's bedroom window. Her drapes and windows were closed. Annie pointed out the flowers that Granny had just planted and the grapevines that her father had planted. She told Thomas about her sisters and brothers and where they lived. Thomas was an only child and he couldn't imagine having so many people under the same roof. Thomas held Annie's hand and looked at her.

**99**

"Annie, you know I never did give you your birthday kiss."

Annie, embarrassed, "I know."

Thomas was a little clumsy, but managed to pull Annie closer to him and kissed her. Annie was wearing a fashion lipstick that looked like shoe polish. From the less affectionate reaction of both Thomas and Annie, it also tasted like shoe polish. They both laughed about the kiss, and they knew then that they would be no more than friends. Annie kept her friendship ring for many years as a remembrance of her "first kiss".

During high school, Annie and Thomas enjoyed going to the WC Handy Theatre to watch movies, and they went to a few house parties together. A couple of times, Annie and two other classmates, danced as "Go-Go" girls in Thomas' small group band at school events.

Thomas made periodic visits to Annie's home with his camera and snapped pictures of her in the back yard, next to Granny's flower garden. They also stayed in touch throughout their adulthood. Annie and Thomas remained good friends forever.

## CHAPTER 20

*Neighborhood Activities*

Within a one mile radius of Annie's house were several small Black owned busi-nesses;

some business owners worked out of their homes. There were several eating places that sold barbeque ribs and links, fried catfish and buffalo fish. But, one of the most frequented restaurants was across from the high school where students bought delicious hamburgers and hotdogs. There was a beauty shop that Annie loved to go to get her hair pressed and curled; barber shop; shoe shop; cleaners; auto repair shop; medical and dental offices and others. One of the greatest spots in the neighborhood was the W.C. Handy Theatre. When black artists came to town, most likely they would perform at the W. C. Handy Theatre. It was built with a stage and booth equipped for small stage performances and movies. Although it was originally built for colored people, the late shows were reserved for white people only. However, during the sixties the Colored people had late shows.

Sometimes Annie, with her siblings and friends, got together to go see the latest movies or performances. She recalled one Saturday when a young man named, Isaac Hayes, and a blues band were scheduled to perform at the theatre. Annie joined Samantha, Claudine and Robert Lee to attend the performances. The theatre was only a mile from the house, thus, they walked. They left a little earlier to get good seats. But, it didn't matter because everybody else was thinking the same and there were long lines. There were no enforced restrictions on the limited capacity of 1,275 seats that existed; tickets were also sold for standing room only. The place was packed. Fortunately, Annie and her siblings arrived on time to get seats.

Once Isaac Hayes sat down at the piano and started singing with that sexy sounding voice, the ladies screamed so loud Annie thought her ears would burst. The young four piece blues band was also awesome. There was no space for dancing, but people danced in their seats. Annie's sister, Samantha, and a few others jumped up on the stage with the band and gave a fantastic dance performance. Annie had a wonderful time and never forgot her experience. A short time later Isaac Hayes became a famous songwriter, singer, musician, and TV and movie actor.

# CHAPTER 21

### The Dentist

Annie started working for a local dentist when she was a junior in high school. Dr. Walter Davis was divorced with two kids; a five year old boy and a six year old girl. He had shared custody of the kids. The days he had them, he needed a baby sitter for a few hours from the time they got out of school until he closed his office. Annie would go to his home after school a couple days out of the week. When he arrived, she would go to her job at a local restaurant.

Dr. Davis was about 35 years old, tall, and fairly attractive. Annie didn't think he was anything real special, but liked that he always spoke kindly to her and appeared to be a gentlemen. He paid her each time she sat for the kids. Annie worked for him for about a year until she was seventeen years old. One evening, when Dr. Davis arrived home, the children were in the den watching TV. Annie gathered her belonging to leave.

"Annie, please help me find my change purse that I misplaced, so I can pay you." Dr. Davis said.

"Okay." Annie replied.

Annie followed him to the back of the house near his bedroom. He turned around, grabbed her and kissed her. Anne felt paralyzed; she had only been kissed once by her friend Thomas. This was different; it was wet and didn't feel good or right. So she pulled back.

"Stop!"

He held her tighter. Annie was wearing a sweater and skirt with socks and laced hush puppies. Dr. Davis placed his hands under skirt and reached into her panties. She didn't want to yell and scare the kids so she tried to fight him off.

"Stop!" Annie pleaded.

He finally had his hand between her legs. When she moved to push him off of her, it opened a space for him to put his finger inside her. She screamed and fought. When he pulled his finger out, there was blood on his hand. He stopped.

"Are you on your period?" He asked Annie.

She pushed him back.

"No." Devastated and in shock, Annie lowered her skirt and went into the bathroom and cried. Dr. Davis knocked on the door to

ask if she was ok.  Annie gathered herself,
opened the door, and headed to the front exit.

"Let me take you to work," Dr. Davis said.

He put the kids in the back seat and they
all rode silently to the restaurant. When the
car stopped, he handed her three dollars for
babysitting.  Annie took the money climbed out
of the car and never spoke to him again.

Annie had befriended one of her co-
workers at the restaurant and came to trust
her. Tearfully, she immediately told her
friend what had happened.

Annie didn't know it, at the time, but
the doctor destroyed her hymen. Annie asked,
"Am I still a virgin?"

# CHAPTER 22

*Tapped Up Shoe*

When Annie got paid from her jobs, her mother insisted that she gave some of the money to her for the family. Annie did as her mother asked. She saved the few remaining dollars for personal hygiene items and her school needs such as shoes, school supplies, and fabric to make clothes. Annie had to save for awhile to have enough money to purchase these items. She did not have a bank account, but placed the money in a metal can and set it on a shelf in the girl's bedroom closet.

Annie's wardrobe consisted of one pair of shoes. Those shoes were for school, work, and church. She had enough outfits to change for one week. As a result, she repeated her outfits until they wore out from washing them frequently. Sometimes, Annie felt blessed when friends or relatives gave her their hand-me-downs. Annie didn't mind wearing used clothes. To her, they were new.

One day after school, Annie rushed home to get some money to purchase a pair of shoes because the shoes she wore that day burst apart from the seams. The next day, she was to meet with a group of classmates for photos. She went to the closet to get her money. When she opened the can only half the money was there. It was not enough to buy the shoes. Annie asked her younger siblings about the money, but each denied knowing anything. Annie was hurt that a family member would steal from her. Unknown to Annie, this had been going on for awhile. Annie didn't usually check the amount in the can, but, she knew how much should have been there.

The next day, Annie showed up at the photo shoot with a taped up shoe. She positioned herself in a manner where the taped shoe could not be seen on the picture. Fortunately, no one noticed or said anything to Annie about her taped shoe.

It would be many years later, when her youngest brother, Aaron, confessed that he and Daisy had stolen her money.

# CHAPTER 23

### *Build A Fence*

There were many churches in Annie's neighborhood. On every other block there stood a church- Baptist, Methodist, Church of Christ, Adventist, Anglican, Lutheran, and Pentecostal. There were about three Baptist churches within one half mile radius. The nearest one to Annie's home was only a few doors down on the same street. Although she went to her mother's Christian Methodist Episcopal Church, she and her siblings enjoyed attending the gospel concerts at the Baptist church. There were male groups that gave great performances.

When Annie was about twelve years old, she began to go to the Baptist church's Sunday morning worships and soon joined the choir. Ms. Ruth was the choir director and pianist. She had the biggest smile and a very strong singing voice. One day she asked Annie to sing a song for the next month's third Sunday service. Annie was so nervous and couldn't understand why anyone would want her to sing anything; especially with no natural singing ability. Annie didn't want to be rude or disrespectful, so she reluctantly agreed.

The song that was chosen was "Jesus, <u>Be</u> a fence all around me," written by Sam Cooke. There were no written instructions during the rehearsals. Annie had to rely on memory and what she heard. What she heard was "<u>Build</u> a fence" and no one told her any different.

The third Sunday came quicker than Annie had hoped. This was her debut as a singer and she was very scared. She sat in the choir stand and didn't hear much of the services because her heart continued to race. Then she heard the music cue; she and the choir stood and sang:

> Jesus build a fence all around me
> everyday
> Jesus I want you to protect me as I travel
> along the way
> I know you can(yes Lord)
> I know you will(yes Lord)
> Fight my battle (yes Lord)
> If I just keep still (yes lord)
> Lord build a fence all around me everyday
>
> This is my prayer Lord that I pray each
> and every day
> That you would guide my footsteps lest I
> stumble and stray
> Lord, I need you to direct me all the way
> long

> Oh Lord build a fence all around me
> everyday
> Come help me say, Jesus...

Annie continued through the end of the song and heard some Amen's from the congregation, especially, when she had some pitch problems. But, she got through it. The church members were polite, yet, she knew singing wasn't her calling. A month later, Annie decided to be baptized in that church.

One evening during choir rehearsal, when Annie was about fourteen years old, she noticed the pastor of the church observing the choir as he sat on one of the member's bench. After the rehearsal, Annie said her goodbyes to everyone and walked towards the exit.

"Miss Annie, do you have a moment?" the pastor called out,

Annie was surprised; but she smiled and walked towards him.

"Yes sir." They stood in front of the podium. He told Annie how well she was doing and asked her a few more questions about school and her family? Then he gave Annie a look that made her very uncomfortable. She looked around the church and noticed that she was alone with

him.  The pastor placed his hand on her breast.
Annie jumped back and landed on the stage.

"I'm not going to hurt you, come here,
you little pretty thang," he said to Annie.

She tried to run towards the exit, but he
blocked her. Annie then ran around the podium
and he ran behind her. She finally jumped down,
ran between the benches, and out the door.
Annie never returned to that church again.

Annie did not tell anyone what had
happened; nor was she aware, at the time, of
how significant the song she learned and sang
in that church, would be to the journeys she
would face in her life.

Annie continued to go to her mother's
church. She always enjoyed hearing her mother
and the gospel choirs sing. The choirs and
worship services were different than the
Baptist church, but they were fulfilling.
Annie was not active in the church, but would
attend various activities with her mother.

At the age of seventeen, after a few
horrendous verbal and physical abusive
experiences, Annie decided to seek spiritual
counsel. One Sunday during the morning
worship, Annie got in line with other members
for the benediction march to shake hands with
the pastor and other elders.

Annie reached out her hand to Pastor Green to shake his hand. She attempted to say something to him; instead, he held on to her hand.

"My wife is at the house, she needs your help on a project, please go on over there," he whispered.

"Yes Sir, I'll go right after services," Annie told him.

She thought, "Oh what a blessing- this is a great opportunity to talk with his wife about my personal issues."

Annie stopped to chat with a few more members before she headed to the church home that was located across the street from the church.

Annie knocked on the door. There was no answer. She knocked once again. Just as she turned to leave, the door opened and it was Pastor Green.

"Come on in Miss Fowler," he said to Annie.

"She's in the back." He pointed in the direction.

Annie walked towards the back room that was a den with a sofa and TV. She stood there waiting to see Mrs. Green. Pastor Green walked up behind Annie.

"Won't you have a seat?" Annie sat down. Pastor Green sat next to her.

"Mrs. Green is not here, I just wanted to see you," he told Annie. Her mind began to scramble and she knew then something was not right.

"What do you mean Pastor Green?" Annie asked.

"You are a beautiful young woman," the pastor said to her. His tone was not one in a clergy manner.

Annie knew what was next. She jumped up and headed to the door. The pastor stood up, but, he did not follow her. Annie let herself out. It would be many years later under a new church leadership before Annie ever visited her mother's church again.

Annie truly felt alone in dealing with life's issues. She had to handle her own business the best she knew how. Annie had no one to turn to, no one she could trust, except Jesus. She thanked God for the comforting words of the song that she was taught. She prayed, "Lord, Build a fence all around me, everyday, and protect me as I travel on my way."

## CHAPTER 24
*What Do They See?*

One Christmas holiday, the family gathered at the Fowler's home. Snow was expected; instead, it was a clear sunny day. A heavy traffic of neighbors and relatives dropped in to give greetings. There was plenty of food; Margaret cooked a turkey and ham with plenty of trimmings and desserts.

"Come on in. Have something to eat. Take what you want, but eat what you take," Jessie greeted and welcomed all of the visitors.

Annie was 17 years old and prayed that she would have help washing the dishes. Several siblings and neighbors were standing on the front porch joking and telling stories. Annie stepped outside to join them.

"Girrrl, you have grown up to be mighty fine. I know you will be breaking hearts," a family friend told Annie.

Annie didn't get a chance to respond when her brother, Junior, made a comment.

"Yeah, she'll be given all that up to get whatever she wants?"

Annie was so hurt and embarrassed. She didn't have the skills or the strength to defend herself. She'd already experienced a traumatic life; twice sexually assaulted as a

**114**

child; been teased and bullied most of her life. She wondered why do people, especially her family, think so little of her and find ways to deliberately hurt her and why they have nothing nice or encouraging to say to her.

"What do they see when they see me?" she asked herself.

## CHAPTER 25

### *The March In Memphis*

Garbage had begun to pile up on the streets throughout the city of Memphis. The beautiful city stunk. Annie had heard about the Sanitation Workers' Strike and she truly sympathized with them. She understood the struggle black people faced with unfair wages. Annie admired the people who were willing to put their lives on the front line for the important cause. Therefore, she decided to march with the strikers, to the city hall, to show her support.

It was a clear and beautiful Friday, February 23, 1968. The publicity of the sanitation strikers caused a lot of tension in the community. Annie and Samantha were at home dressing to go downtown to the sanitation march.

"You better stay home. It is crazy out there. You cannot go to the march," Margaret told them.

The girls assured their mother that they would be fine and that they must go.

"If you leave this house you will get a beaten," Margaret threatened as the girls walked out the door. But they went anyway.

Annie knew their mother was frightened for her children.

When Annie and Samantha arrived at the marcher's line up location, the striker's leaders informed everyone about what to do during a peaceful march. As they lined up, Annie noticed her best friend Leola and her mother were already in line. It felt good to Annie to see them there. Annie carried a sign that said "Fair and Equal Wages". Samantha carried one similar. They kept up with the marchers and stayed calm. About fifteen minutes into the march, Annie saw people running back. Soon there were dogs barking and people screaming. Leola and her mother turned and ran very fast. Annie followed. She barely kept up with Leola's mother who was running faster than she. They continued to run until they felt safer. Annie and Samantha got separated. Annie looked back at the people; some were still running, others washed mace from their eyes with water, some had blood on their legs from falling or dog bites, some were crying and some cursed.

Annie soon returned home and watched the news with the family. Samantha later called home to say she was in jail. She had always been a jokester, so she recanted when she could hear their mother's voice with concern and fear. Samantha had not been jailed; she was safe at a friend's home.

Margaret didn't beat any of her children that night; she was relieved that they were all safe.

Martin Luther King, Jr. (MLK) took a great interest in the sanitation workers' cause. He agreed to come and support the marchers. When he arrived there was a lot of violence and a curfew was in placed. Annie and the family stayed near the TV to keep abreast of what was going on. What was so hard for Annie to understand was: why did the marchers destroy their own community? MLK still spoke at a church asking for a peaceful march. He promised to return in April to participate in the peaceful march.

Later on Wednesday, April 3, 1968, Annie rushed home from school. She knew that Martin Luther King, Jr. was in Memphis to speak at Mason Temple Church. A neighbor, Brenda, had planned to drive there and offered Annie a ride. After Annie finished her chores, she put on her church clothes and got ready to leave. Wednesdays was also a choir rehearsal night for Margaret and she was getting dressed to go to her church. Margaret was tearful as she watched Annie, but didn't try to stop her.

"Goodbye Mother, I'll come home right after church," Annie said.

The traffic was heavy as Annie and the car load of neighbors approached the church. Brenda parked the car a few blocks away and they had to walk to the church. There were long lines of people moving slowly to the entrance of the church doors. Annie and her neighbors got in line. Annie noticed the people dressed in their Sunday best and some dressed in African attire. It was a peaceful and calm evening. Annie was very close to the entrance doors when she heard,

"Sorry there is no more room in the church."

Annie looked toward the rear of her and saw there were still long lines of people. No one left after the announcement. The doors were left open so that the people waiting could hear his voice. Martin's voice was uplifting as he began his speech, "I've been to the Mountaintop". Everyone was captivated by every word he spoke. For forty four minutes, no one moved, nor left until after his last word. Everyone gave him praises.

Annie was disappointed that she didn't get to see MLK, but she thought his voice would echo in her heart forever.

When Annie arrived home, her mother had not gotten home yet. After choir rehearsal,

Margaret and her best friend usually stopped by Lobes Barbeque take-out to pick up some pork skins. Sure enough, Margaret came home with a greasy bag of pork skins. She seemed relieved to see Annie there. The two sat down at the kitchen table and talked about the speech while snacking on the skins.

The next day, Annie went to school excited to share stories with her classmates about MLK's speech and all that she saw. The day was a good day for Annie. She arrived home from work about 7pm. When she entered the door, Margaret had tears in her eyes and was singing. Annie stood and listened to her mother for a moment.

"Just a closer walk with Thee,
Grant it, Jesus, is my plea,
Daily walking close to Thee,
Let it be, dear Lord, let it be."

The younger siblings ran out of their room and shouted, "They killed Martin Luther King." Annie fell on her knees and cried,          "Why is there so much hate? Why?"

"Through this world of toil and snares,
If I falter, Lord, who cares?
Who with me my burden shares?
None but Thee, dear Lord, none but Thee."
Margaret sang.

**120**

## CHAPTER 26

*Senior Year*

Senior year came too quickly for Annie. She had settled into a welcoming family-like environment with her classmates that she truly loved. Annie didn't want to look ahead and think about never coming on campus again as a student.

Annie's parents didn't verbally push her to make good grades. She thought they definitely wanted her to complete her education, but, she wasn't sure how far they expected her to go. Jessie's rule for his children that stuck in Annie's head was, "You have to leave my house by age 18."

With only a 2.6 GPA out of 4.0, Annie's grades were not good enough to receive an academic scholarship, hence she didn't know for sure what she wanted; or would be able to do. Annie had taken advantage of all the vocational and occupational classes that included a bookkeeping course offered at the high school and she did well in them.

Her family member's lively-hood and careers centered on military, ministries, domestic work, construction, and medical assistance experiences. Annie wasn't interested in any of those areas to work.

Although she loved the performing arts, she felt that she didn't have the natural skills or talent to make it a practical profession.

During the last semester of her senior year, Annie stopped working at the restaurant and started a job in Dr. Young's neighborhood family medical office. Annie was trained to give injections/shots to patients, and to handle general office work. Dr. Young was a kind man who was in his forties. He was a bit shocked at the questions Annie asked about caring for her body during menstruation. Especially, since Annie had recently turned 18 years old. He gave her advice and products should she decide to use them. Annie enjoyed working with the patients and thought she might like the nursing profession.

During that time, Margaret's brother, Uncle Shooey, worked at a Historical Black College/University (HBCU), in Nashville, TN. Since Annie didn't have the appropriate GPA for an academic scholarship, Uncle Shooey suggested to Annie that she apply for a work-study scholarship at the university. He also offered to take her to visit the campus and to talk with one of the counselors. Annie graciously accepted and invited her best friend, Leola, to go with her to Nashville to apply for entrance into a program. Uncle Shooey drove Annie and Leola to the university and showed them the campus. Initially, neither knew exactly what they wanted to major in. But, by the end of their visit at the university, Annie decided nursing and Leola decided business education.

The heart breaking death of MLK was still felt in the community and at school during the last semester. None of Annie secret admirers invited her to the high school senior prom. For this reason, Annie asked a distant maternal cousin, Bookie, who was also her classmate and a football player, to go to the prom with her. Bookie had a wonderful personality and kind heart. Annie and Bookie had an amazing time.

Many years after graduation, her admirers confessed to Annie that they thought Annie had already been asked to the prom and they feared her rejection.

## CHAPTER 27

### The Summer Of 1968

Annie's oldest sister Elaine, who lived in Oregon, came to visit the family during the July 4ᵗʰ holiday. Annie truly loved her sister and trusted everything she said. During her visit, Elaine invited Annie to a James Brown Concert in downtown Memphis. Annie felt so happy that Elaine asked her.

Annie wore the latest 70's fashion and added a long thick pony tail to finish the look. Elaine wore a mini dress and sandal toe shoes will large earrings. A relative dropped Elaine and Annie off at the downtown coliseum.

James Brown gave a magnificent performance to a sold out crowd. He was having so much fun that he stayed a little longer than planned.

After the show, Annie and Elaine walked through the heavy crowd to find a taxi. After about five minutes of flagging for a taxi, a police officer came up to them.

"Are you having trouble getting a taxi?" he and asked them.

"Yes, I guess it is a very busy night." Elaine smiled and said.

Annie stood and observed.

"I'm Floyd Hightower, I'm coming off duty and I'll be happy to take you both to your home.

Elaine looked at Annie who was still observing.

"Oka, we would really appreciate that," Elaine smiled.

Annie and Elaine remained standing in the same spot while Floyd retrieved his car. Moments later, a new 1968 black Pontiac Firebird stopped in front of them. Floyd got out and let the ladies in. Annie sat in the tight fitting back seat and Elaine sat up front. Floyd was a nice looking man. His uniform was well pressed and fitted to perfection. Annie noticed that he had a similar built and complexion as her father. He had nice brown eyes and thick kinky-curly dark brown hair. He was about twenty five years old, which seemed old to Annie. When Floyd reached the house he stopped, hopped out of the car and opened the doors for the ladies. Elaine whispered to Annie to get his phone number. Annie wondered why Elaine wanted his number, since she was a married woman. Annie had no intentions of asking for his number. Floyd walked the ladies to the door. He reached out his hand towards Annie to give her a piece of paper.

"Please call me sometimes" he said.

Annie took the paper with no intention of calling him. She thanked him for the ride and she and Elaine went inside the house.

Elaine continued the conversation.

"Girl, he looks like a taker. He's a gentleman, good looking and seemed like a good age for you."

"I'm about to leave for college and I don't want anything serious," Annie responded.

"Well you have about two more months before you leave, you should try to get to know him," Elaine said.

Annie still did not call Floyd. But a few days later, he knocked on her parent's door. He wasn't in uniformed and looked different. He had a nice smile, small waistline, muscular built, and a cute round butt. Elaine was still visiting and had planned to leave the following day. She saw Floyd at the door and asked him to come in. She offered him some water, made small talk and left him in the living room with Annie.

Floyd started talking about the different neighborhoods and how fast they were growing. During their conversations, Annie noticed that Floyd had the same problem she had as a little girl. He had difficulty pronouncing words beginning with "S" and "Th". He would say "screet" for street, and "dat" for that. She thought it would be inappropriate or might embarrass him if she shared her experience with the speech therapist. Although, she wondered why he didn't receive speech therapy, she later realized that the educational system for black students was far less equal to the educational system for white and military students.

Annie had considered what her sister had said to her about getting to know Floyd and she began to loosen up. They chatted for a few minutes and he asked for Annie's phone number. She gave it to him.

Floyd called Annie every day. She finally invited him to drop by the house while her mother and father were present. He was a perfect gentleman during his visit. Margaret was very pleasant towards him and seemed to like him. Jessie was cautious as usual.

A few times Floyd came by with his full uniform including his guns. Jessie didn't like guns in his house and asked Annie to talk to Floyd about it. Annie did talk to Floyd about it and he never wore his uniform to the house again.

Annie learned that Floyd had been on the police force for about three years and he was also a motorcycled police officer. He joined the police academy soon after he left the US Marines. His last duty was actual combat in Vietnam for eighteen months.

Annie went out on a few dates with Floyd. He took her out to dinner and to a night club. Floyd drank alcohol and Annie didn't. Since she loved lemony flavored drinks, she ordered a seven-up soda. She had never drank alcohol nor been to a night club before. But, she did love to dance. Floyd wasn't crazy about dancing, but tried his awkward moves on the floor.

Floyd took Annie to visit his twin sisters who were very warm and caring people. The sisters had lived together most of their lives and were not married. Floyd came from a family of sixteen children. His father had passed away, but his mother was still living in the same country town where he was born.

One day Floyd took Annie to meet his mother. She was a pleasant woman, but didn't care for the new fashion of short skirts. Annie didn't pick up the jest his mother made about her skirt, but Floyd did and he didn't like it. However, Annie did pick up a little tension between them. She didn't think much about it, especially, having come from a dysfunctional family herself.

One day, Floyd drove his motorcycle over to the Annie's house and offered to take her for a ride. Annie had never been on a motorcycle before, but was excited about the opportunity. Annie dressed in a pair of walking shorts with a blouse and flat shoes. Neither one wore a helmet. She was nervous and asked him not to take her too far. Floyd agreed and she hopped on behind him. He roared the motor and off they went. Floyd took her around the corner to her Uncle John's (Jessie's youngest brother) house. Annie asked Floyd to stop the motorcycle. Floyd pulled into her uncle's driveway. A couple of cousins were outside and went over to talk to Annie. They thought the bike was cool. Annie got off the cycle to speak with them for a moment and made introductions. She attempted to hop back on the cycle when her leg brushed against the hot pipe on the motorcycle. The burn was pretty painful, but Annie didn't want to make a fuss about it. Floyd took Annie back home and suggested that she put some ice on it. There was no ice; instead, Annie placed a cool wet cloth on it. The burn left a second degree scar. Needless to say, Annie never rode the motorcycle again.

A few days later, Annie had a menstrual period and felt very ill. When Floyd called, she was unable to talk with him. She just wanted to sleep, but instead she vomited over and over again for hours. Jessie and Margaret took her to the military hospital to get some codeine medication for relief. Annie came back home and slept until the next day.

When Annie finally saw, Floyd, he asked her a lot of questions about her illness. When he learned it was just a bad monthly period he seemed to be relieved and mentioned that one of his sisters had the same problem. He asked Annie the strangest question.

"Are you regular?"

Annie was not sure of the question.

"What do you mean?" she asked.

"Do you know exactly when this will happen again?" he asked.

Curiously, Annie looked at him.

"Yes." Is that what you meant by regular?" Floyd nodded.

Annie had never received so much attention from anyone. She was beginning to enjoy Floyd's company and felt safe with him. About a week later, Floyd took Annie to a movie. After they left the movie, he took her by his house. He lived in a one bedroom shot-gun duplex. He introduced Annie to one of his distant cousins and her husband who lived in the duplex on the other side of his. Floyd showed Annie the inside of his home. The first room was the living room; the next room was a room that could be a dining room or another bedroom; next was the kitchen and the last rooms were the bedroom and bathroom.

The dinner Floyd cooked included cream corn, cornbread, chicken and a cucumber and tomato salad. Annie saw the freshly made lemonade and was happy that Floyd remembered she loved lemony drinks. Annie wasn't too fond of the cuisine, but acted very surprised and gracious. They sat down to eat. Annie had noticed before that Floyd did not say a blessing before eating food. So this time, she decided to say the same blessing as her father. Floyd paused and when Annie finished, he said, "Amen." For dessert, Floyd offered Annie ice cream. She refused.

"You eat 'bout as much as a bird," he told her.

After dinner, they moved to the front living room. Floyd turned on the TV with the sound turned down, and turned on the radio to soft R&B music. They both sat on the sofa. When Floyd moved close to Annie, she let him kiss her. He held her tight and gave her a long passionate kiss. He was sweaty with an erection and kissed her again. Annie kissed him back; in her mind she thought about what her girlfriend had told her about kissing.

After the terrible first kiss with her friend Thomas, Annie asked her friend Carmela about kissing. To Annie, Carmela seemed so knowledgeable about many topics. She was an only child for several years before her younger siblings were born. Carmela seemed to have adult wisdom all her life. There were times when Carmela question Annie's behavior on issues and she provided information to Annie that changed Annie for the better.

Carmela told Annie how to kiss a man with the rolling of the tongue. She told Annie;

"You don't give too much tongue if you are not yet in love."

When Annie kissed Floyd, she didn't give him any tongue. She wasn't feeling the love, and felt he needed a bit more work on his personal hygiene. But, she truly cared for him.

About a week later, Floyd picked up Annie from her job and took her out for dinner and dancing at a night club.

Floyd handed Annie a drink.

"What is it?" Annie asked Floyd.

"Just taste it -you will like it."
Annie took a sip. It was very lemony with a
little sweetness. It tested pretty well to
Annie. She said,

"What is it called?" She asked.

"It's the whisky sour mix, but it has
very little alcohol," Floyd explained.

Annie continued to sip. By the end of
the date she had three drinks. Annie was
felt weird, she slurred her words, giggled
and she felt horny.

Later, Floyd took Annie to his house.
Annie wasn't sure what was going on, but she
did not resist. They had sex. It was a new
experience. Annie was extremely tight and it
was painful. Floyd had a large penis that made
it difficult for him to fit inside of her, but
he did. Floyd reached a climax. Annie was
silent. She laid there a little longer then
asked Floyd to take her home.

It was after 2a.m. when Annie arrived
home. Margaret opened the door to let her in.
Margaret didn't say anything. Annie went
straight to bed. She laid in bed for a few
minutes, then prayed that she was not pregnant
and soon fell asleep.

Annie had about three weeks before she would leave for Nashville. She continued to work and went out on dates with Floyd.

About a week before her departure, Annie monthly period was late. She didn't know what to do. When she went to work the next day she talked to Dr. Young and told him she might be pregnant.

"You might not be- it could be a delay because of the stress you've been under. I can give you a shot that would help your period come on only if you are not pregnant," he told Annie.

She agreed to take the shot. He also drew blood for a pregnancy test; but, the test results would take about two weeks.

Meanwhile, a couple of days later, Annie had to use the bathroom really badly and her mother was in the bathroom, but let Annie inside. While Annie set on the toilet and did her business, Margaret stood in front of the sink looking in the mirror. "Why haven't you had your period?" Margaret asked,

She was surprised by the question.

"Oh, I still have time," Annie lied.

Margaret said no more.

The very next day, Floyd asked Annie the same question her mother had asked? Annie felt like everyone was spying on her and everyone in the world knew about her periods.

"Annie did you take a test?" Floyd asked.

"My boss took my blood for a test, but I will have to wait two weeks for the results," she told him.

Annie packed her bags and was ready to go to college. Jessie, Margaret, Janis, Aaron, and Martha, all got in the car with Annie for the three hour drive to Nashville. Annie thought about how disappointed her parents would be if she was pregnant.

When Jessie arrived on campus, Annie could see the pride on her father's face. Everyone helped Annie to her dorm. They laid down her boxes and suitcases. Afterwards, Annie gave them a tour of the campus before they headed back to Memphis.

Jessie gave Annie a tight hug. Her heart ached. Margaret did the same and the siblings followed. Annie watched them drive off until they disappeared. She felt so lost.

The first few weeks went well. Annie had forgotten about her situation and focused on acclimating and getting her course schedule completed. As part of the work-study program, Annie started to work at the college book store as a clerk. She joined the band and was elected Miss Band.

Annie had not contacted Dr. Young about her blood test results. She was in denial. She kept putting it off. She had not spoken to Floyd.

About two days later, she was contacted by the administration that she had a visitor. Floyd had arrived on campus.

Annie met Floyd on the lawn in front of her dorm.  He smiled when he saw Annie and he gave her a hug and kiss.  They sat down on the bench. Floyd got straight to the point.

"Hey Annie, hope you are feeling well. I got your results from the doctor. You are pregnant and we should get marry."

Annie just stared.  This was not the type of marriage proposal Annie had dreamt about. *Her knight in shining armor kneels before her, and tells her how much he loves her, and can't live without her. He pulls out a ring and asks her to marry him.*

Floyd continued.

"I told your father you were pregnant, and he got upset.  But, I told him I love you."

Annie had been silent, but got upset.

"You did what? How did you get my blood test? Why did you tell my father?"

Floyd pulled out a ring box; took the ring out of the box and placed it on Annie's finger.

"Please think about it," he asked. They sat in silence for while. Floyd finally left to drive back to Memphis. Annie was left with a lot to think about.

## CHAPTER 28

*Forward To Present Day 2014*

Annie was tearful as she thought about how the first eight months of 1968 took a turn in her life in all directions. In that short period, Annie was a senior in high school and participated in a human rights event that would be an important part of the world's history; graduated from high school; had sex for the first time; went to college; discovered she's pregnant; and now she had to decide if she wanted to marry a man she only knew for three months.

Annie wiped her eyes, looked down at the album in her lap, and ran her fingers across a photo of her and Floyd on their wedding day.

# CHAPTER 29

## *The Wedding*

On a Friday evening, Annie caught a Greyhound bus and headed to Memphis. She didn't know what she was going to say to Jessie, but she was going back to plan a wedding.

Annie's sister, Claudine, had gotten married earlier that year in March. Annie was the maid of honor, and since Claudine lived out of town, she agreed to orchestrate the wedding for Claudine. The wedding was held at Margaret's church. Annie and Margaret worked very hard for Claudine to have a perfect wedding. Margaret made the bride's dress. Annie gathered a few of her friends to be in the wedding as bridesmaids. Her friends bought the fabric and Margaret and Annie made the dresses. Claudine did very little; just showed up. It was a beautiful wedding held at Margaret's church.

Annie's wedding was set for October 15, less than a month away. This meant Jessie will have given away two daughters within seven months. Annie remained in college for the semester and had only the weekends to work on the wedding. Although she felt a bit tired from pregnancy, Annie decided to ride the greyhound

**139**

round-trip each weekend. Sometimes Floyd drove her back to the campus.

There was very little money to spend. Hence, Margaret asked Claudine to allow Annie to wear her wedding dress. Claudine agreed. She was a size larger than Annie, but Margaret made it work. Annie asked her same friends that were in her sister's wedding to be in her wedding. They agreed to buy the fabric and Annie and Margaret made the dresses.

Everyone accepted Floyd's suggestion to have the wedding at his mother's church. Since it was fall, Annie decided apple green for the bridal color with red roses as the bridal bouquets. Floyd's twin sisters were so kind and helpful during the entire process. Since they were seamstresses, they made Annie an ivory two piece suit and an apple green blouse to wear at the reception. They also included a cute large apple green ribbon bow with pearls for Annie's hair. Margaret made Annie a striking long veil of pearls and lace that matched her wedding dress perfectly.

Floyd's family agreed to prepare the food for the reception that would be held in the basement of the church, and to make arrangements with the minister.

Annie and Floyd did not have any pre-wedding counseling. There was no bridal party. The wedding day arrived.

It was a sunny day. The church was modestly decorated and looked very nice. Annie's brother, Donny, was at the door as an usher. He looked very handsome in his dark suit and tie. Margaret was glowing in her self-made cream color two piece laced suit with a matching hat. Margaret's mother also attended the wedding. As usual, Mamma McGwin looked eloquent. The groom and groomsmen were standing place. Floyd looked very special in his black tuxedo.

Annie had not seen the decorations yet. She left school the day before and had just made it on time for the rehearsal. With very little sleep, she could barely get up that morning. She was so filled with doubt and wandered:

*"Why am I doing this? Why don't Daddy and Mother tell me I don't have to get married? Who is this man I'm marrying? I've only known him for three month."*

The beautiful bridesmaids and maid of honor had walked down the aisle and taken their places. The little flower girl was standing in front of Annie and Jessie was waiting to walk her down the aisle.

Annie heard her cue. She looked into her father's eyes— she saw sadness in them, but he smiled; then she walked towards him. He held his arm out to her; Annie's mind snapped into a fairytale mode: *She is the princess and her father, the king, is giving her away to a wonderful and handsome prince.*

Annie was eight weeks pregnant, but she showed no signs. She sparkled as she walked down the aisle with her father and smiled at everyone. She looked so beautiful.

The photographer was on a tight schedule and he needed to take the pictures immediately after the wedding and before the reception. The wedding party and the immediate family remained in the sanctuary. The photos shoot went well, but a little longer than expected.

Annie, Floyd and the rest of party headed down to the basement to the reception. Everyone was seated and eating. Annie and Floyd sat down and waited to be served. They waited and they waited. Soon Floyd got up to see why the holdup. About the same time, the photographer approached Annie to let her know it was time to take a picture with the cake. Floyd returned not smiling. Annie led him to the cake.

"What's wrong?" she asked him.

"They ate the food, and didn't save us anything. Let's cut this damn cake and get out of here." he whispered.

Annie, Floyd and some of the bridal parties met at a night club. The club didn't have a full menu, but there was plenty of food; fried chicken, biscuits, cold slaw and drinks. The music was nice and several people danced. However, the tired little princess slept through the entire reception.

Floyd drove Annie back to college. On the way, Annie had an epiphany; when she visited her parent's home, Annie knew at a glance that something was different about the front of the house. But, it wasn't until that moment that she realized that the large oak tree that was in the front yard had been cut down.

The oak tree was Annie's retreat and sanctuary, as a young girl. She had a favorite branch that she would sit on to watch the pass-a-byes; to daydream; or just to escape. The tree now gone made Annie leaving home feel real.

# CHAPTER 30

## *Back To College*

The honeymoon was postponed for the Thanksgiving break. The next day, Annie headed back to school. The college's band was getting ready for the homecoming parade. They wanted Annie to ride in a decorated convertible. She was excited about being the band's queen and wrote to tell Floyd about it in hope that he would come up to watch the parade.

The parade was on a Saturday; Floyd made a surprised visit that Friday evening before. Annie was glad to see Floyd. But, he had an air about him that Annie had not seen before.

"You are a married and pregnant woman now. You can't be riding in no parade," he said to her.

Annie, not understanding, "I'm not showing and it won't hurt the baby."

"It don't matter. You are my wife," he argued.

Annie clearly understood it was all about possession.

Annie was taken aback about the conversation and Floyd's demands. However, she decided not to ride in the parade.

Annie continued going to her classes and working in the bookstore. She made a few friends in the dorm who were very supportive of her and knew that she was married and pregnant.

It was the week before the Thanksgiving weekend and Annie was looking forward to her honeymoon trip to Chattanooga, Tennessee. Therefore, she worked extra hard to catch up with all her course work. By the end of the week, Annie had completed all the assign-ments and was free to leave a day earlier than planned. So, Annie decided to surprise Floyd by getting to Memphis the day before.

Annie had arranged for her cousin, Bill, to give her a lift to her house and he was waiting at the bus station when she arrived in Memphis. They drove straight to the house. Annie didn't see Floyd's car, so she used her key to let herself in. After Bill saw that she was safe, he said goodbye and left.

The house was in an unusual mess. Clothes and shoes were in the living room. Dirty dishes were on the table and in the sink. The bed was not made. Annie looked closer at the bed; the pillow case seemed wet. She touched it- and it was wet. Then she pulled the top sheet back and noticed the bottom sheet was also wet. There was a small towel on the floor next to the bed.

Annie walked back to the kitchen and began clearing the table and the dishes. She noticed lipstick on one of the glasses. At that point, a lot of things were running through her head. *(I know that fool is not cheating on me, we just got married. There must be a logical reason for this. I'll just wait to see what he has to say about it.)*

About an hour later Floyd arrived, surprised to see Annie.

"Hey, when did you get here? I was expecting you tomorrow," he said.

"I decided to come earlier, thought I would surprise you," Annie replied.

"Well, you did," he hesitated.

"Who's been here?" she asked.

"What do you mean?" Floyd looked curious.

"There are dishes with lipstick, and the bed is wet," she insisted.

"Uh Uh Oh that. Well, I let my little brother use the house, while I was at work."

"What do you mean use- isn't this our home?" Annie asked.

"Yeah, but I won't let him do it again,"
replied Floyd.

Annie accepted Floyd's answers, but was
not satisfied; deep in her soul she felt
something wasn't right.

A couple of days later, Annie and Floyd
headed to Chattanooga on their honeymoon. This
was Annie's first trip there. Floyd reserved
a room at a hotel that recently allowed black
people to patronize. The room was nice. They
arrived in time to have dinner and to make
plans for the next day. Annie was about 14
weeks pregnant and still had a flat stomach.
She did like the little weight gained on the
butt and Floyd seemed to like it too. Annie
was a bit too tired to make love, but Floyd
was ready and she abided. Annie had decided
to make a good life with Floyd and to be loyal
to him. She wanted to be the best wife to him
and the greatest mom to their unborn child.
She hoped Floyd felt the same.

The next day Annie and Floyd spent the
day at the attractions. She enjoyed the Lookout
Mountain, Ruby Falls, Rock City, the Inclined
Railroad, and Lovers' Leap. They stayed
another two days and headed back to Memphis to
spend time with the family for the Thanksgiving
holidays.

Annie spent time with her family as well as Floyd's. There was a lot of food choices; and much family laughter. It was a wonderful holiday.

Annie returned to the university feeling inspired and had accepted her fate as a wife and an expectant mother. She enjoyed her classes and playing the flute in the band. She looked forward to seeing Floyd and her family again during the Christmas holidays.

Annie only returned once to Memphis between the holidays. She had a lot of papers to complete and was still working at the bookstore. The semester would not end until the middle of January. This meant that Annie would have to return to the campus after Christmas and New Year, before she would official complete the semester.

The Christmas holiday was much like Thanksgiving, except for the gift giving. All of Annie's siblings were at home for a visit. Jessie and Margaret seemed so happy. Annie was about eighteen weeks and showed a small bump. She and the baby were doing well. It was a wonderful time for Annie.

# CHAPTER 31

### *Making a Home*

Once back in Memphis, Annie put all her energy in making their home comfortable and clean. Annie had developed a mild case of obsessive compulsive disorder (OCD) that she believed she inherited from Jessie. She recalled when living in Missouri and Jessie was in charge of the military mass hall, he invited the children to the cafeteria. He pointed out how clean things were (like the walls, stoves and fridges) and how hard it was to keep it clean. Jessie had received Commendations for his great leadership in maintaining the mess hall. Apparently, Annie was the only child that followed Jessie's footsteps.

When Jessie came home from work he expected the house to be just as clean. But Margaret didn't take it that seriously. She liked a lived-in-house; so a little dirt and messiness were okay with her. Each time the family moved to a new location, Jessie made everyone scrub the walls, boards, and floors until it met his approval.

Now that Annie was in her own home, she wanted a clean and healthy environment. Sometimes, pregnant Annie got on her knees to clean the floors to her approval. She cooked, but Floyd had to adjust to some of her cooking because he preferred more salt and starches. Annie would try her best to accommodate him.

When Floyd came home, the house was clean and organized, and the food was prepared.

Annie was almost nineteen years old and didn't have her driver's license. Floyd had replaced his firebird with a blue Volkswagen Bug with standard shifts. It was the only transportation between them. Annie wanted to be able to do more errands instead of waiting on Floyd to get home.

Annie watched Floyd each time he drove the bug. She noticed the clutch movement with the change in gears; the acceleration of the gas paddle; when he stopped and changed the gears. In her head she felt she had it together.

One day Floyd came home early during the day and went straight to bed. Annie was bored with nothing to do. She took Floyd's keys and took the car for a drive. Annie felt so confident that she drove it to a nearby cousin's house. After a short visit she headed home. She surprised herself on how well she had done. Annie parked the car in front of the house and thought about what she was going to say to Floyd about getting her driver's license.

When Annie entered the house Jessie was awake and sitting on the sofa in the living room watching TV. "Oh Lord," she thought to herself, but was surprised as to how calmed he was. She told him what she had done. About a week later, Floyd took Annie to the DMV to get her driver's license. But, he would never let Annie drive while he was in the car.

It was Saturday, March 1, 1969 and Annie turned 19 years old. Floyd had left early for work and left a note he would be home about 7:30pm. It was about 8 a.m. when the phone rang. Samantha called to wish Annie a happy birthday. Samantha was good about remembering everybody's birthdays and anniversaries. She put Margaret on the phone to express the same wishes. Margaret also invited Annie to come over for lunch. Annie accepted. The phone rang about ten times with the happy birthday wishes. It made Annie feel special. But she hadn't heard from Floyd.

"Maybe he got busy with police business," she thought.

Annie's bump was showing and she was moving a little slower. She was about 30 weeks pregnant and had about 10 weeks to go. She ate and got dressed. She made up the bed and went through the house to make sure the house was in order. Annie did not like coming home to a messy house.

Annie's sister, Samantha asked one of her friends to pick up Annie. When Annie opened the door to her parent's home, she could smell the aroma of delicious foods. Samantha and Margaret had been cooking and Jessie was in the back yard cooking on the grill. That was the only cooking Jessie did. He made the barbeque sauce, mayo and mustard from scratch; and made it as spicy hot as desired.

Several relatives and friends arrived. Some of them Annie hadn't seen for a very long time. The day was wonderful and it made her feel good to be at home again.

The house was soon full and everyone ate. To walk off all the food she had eaten, Annie walked through the neighborhood and stopped to visit a few of them. She soon returned to the house and received a phone message from Floyd saying that he would pickup Annie.

Annie thanked her family for their thoughtfulness and the good food. It had been a long afternoon for Annie and she was feeling tired. Floyd finally showed up and he accepted a plate to go. They drove back to their place.

Floyd unlocked the door with his key and stepped inside before Annie to turn on the lights. Once Annie stepped in the door Floyd flipped the light switch. And several people screamed,

"Surprise!!!!" Several people shouted.

Annie screamed so loud they got a little scared for her. When they saw she was okay, they all laughed – so did Annie.

Floyd had planned the surprise for Annie all week. Most of his relatives and friends were there; some of them Annie had never met. She managed to work her way through the small and crowed space. Annie thanked everyone.

"So you're legal now," One person said to Annie.

"How does it feel to be a legal age?"

Annie was confused.

"I am 19 years old," she replied.

Some of them looked away and a few looked at each other. Apparently, Floyd had told them that Annie was 21 years old.

There was light food, sodas, alcohol and a nice chocolate cake; Floyd's favorite. Annie was too full to eat anything, but she drank a club soda. The guests didn't stay too long. By the time the last guest left, Annie couldn't keep her eyes open.

"Thank you Floyd for the wonderful surprise. I really enjoyed everything." Annie kissed Floyd.

Annie showered and went to bed; she was in a deep sleep before her head hit the pillow.

When Annie woke up, it was morning. Floyd was up and in the kitchen eating breakfast. Annie put on a robe and went into the kitchen. She said, "good morning" and gave him a kiss. She placed a prenatal vitamin in her mouth and washed it down with water. She then ate some eggs and toast. Floyd had walked to the front room.

"Hey Annie come here. I need to show you something," Floyd called out.

Annie got little concerned.

"What is it?"

"It's outside," he said.

"Do I need to put on some clothes?" she asked.

"It won't take but a minute. Come on," Floyd insisted.

Annie followed him outside and saw a 1965 Rambler Convertible parked next to the VW Bug, but thought nothing of it.

"Well?" Floyd asked.

Annie looked at Floyd and then looked at the car and squealed. She ran around the car in her robe.

"For me?  Oh my goodness. Thank you, honey. Thank you. When can we take it for a ride?" she pleaded.

"As soon as you put some clothes on," Floyd said, smiling.

The following day Annie took another ride in her new car. This time, she spent the whole day making short stops at her parents, relatives and friends.

# CHAPTER 32

### *Unbelievable*

Annie had been in her new life environment for only three months when she started to receive hang-up phone calls. She noticed that when Floyd was home and she answered the phone, the caller hung up. But minutes after the phone would ring, Floyd answered, he would whisper a few words and hang up. She also noticed Floyd stayed away from home longer periods of time. There were times Floyd did not come home for two or three days. Annie remained in denial that her husband was cheating and continued her regular daily routine.

One day Floyd was driving Annie back to the house from a doctor's appointment. Annie was about two weeks from delivery and the doctor had told them that Annie will have to have a caesarian birth. He explained to them that the baby was too large for normal birth, but Annie would still have to wait for the labor to begin.

During the drive, Annie asked Floyd if he was going to be able to take some time off after the baby was born. He did not reply. Annoyed by his lack of response, Annie continued, "I'll need you…" Before she could speak another word, she felt a great force across her face that caused her to see lights.

Floyd had back handed her. Annie was surprised, shock and hurt. She started crying and screaming for him to stop the car and let her out. Floyd threatened to hit her again if she didn't shut up and kept driving until he reached their house. He pulled Annie out of the car and forced her inside the house. He punched her in the head a couple more time. Annie rolled in a fetal position protecting her head and the baby. When she thought he was finished, Annie got off the floor and sat down on the sofa. She thought about ways to get out of the house. But, he wouldn't let her leave his sight.

"You're not going nowhere."

Floyd pulled Annie to the back bedroom and shut the door. Annie cried so hard, she fell asleep from exhaustion. Floyd slept a few hours in the living room, but he had to get ready for work. He carried on as if nothing had happen. Floyd opened the door to the bedroom and asked Annie if she wanted something to eat. Annie refused. When he finished dressing he returned to the bedroom, kissed her on her forehead and told her he would come straight home after work. Annie nodded. Floyd left for work.

Annie waited a few minutes then got up and showered. There were no noticeable bruises on her face. But her head ached badly. She got dressed and didn't bother to eat; she grabbed her purse and the keys to her car and left the house. Once she got in the car, she stuck the key in the ignition, but it would not start. It didn't make a noise. She tried several times before she understood that Floyd had done something to the car. He had removed the starter. Annie went back into the house to call her cousin, Tamera, to pick up her at another location. Annie took a bus to that location and Tamera was waiting. Tamera drove Annie to her parents' house.

The moment Margaret saw Annie, she knew something was wrong. She offered Annie something to eat. Annie ate eggs, toast, bacon, and a small bowl of oatmeal; she didn't realize how hungry she was. Margaret asked Annie if she was okay. Annie told her she had a bad headache and she wanted to lie down. So she did. Annie felt better in a few hours and went up front where Jessie was. Her mother told her she had a phone call; it was Floyd. Annie took the call.

"Annie come back home," he pleaded.

"Don't you dare come over here! I need time."

She sat down on the sofa. Jessie had been sitting there in his chair and over heard the

**158**

conversation. Jessie, was a man of few words, but he could see that Annie was troubled.

"You are about to go in labor and you don't what to go home, why?" he asked her.

Annie looked at her father about her reply and thought;

"How do I tell a man who beats his wife and children the truth?" So, Annie lied.

"Well, you know how a man gets jealous of his wife; sometimes they get crazy."

"No I don't know, because Margaret is the jealous one -not me," Jessie responded.

With that response, Annie was glad she didn't tell her father the truth.

Annie stayed a couple of nights with her parents. Floyd came over and they had a conversation in the backyard. Floyd pleaded with Annie and when that didn't work he cried. Annie had never seen a grown man cry. It was a turn off to her, especially in this situation. It wasn't as if he was physically hurt or someone died.

She and her sibling mocked and laughed at one another when the other cried; so the first thing Annie did was laughed. That surprised Floyd.

"I promise Annie, I will never hit you again."

Annie went back home with Floyd, but she still had concerns about trusting Floyd.

# CHAPTER 33

## *New Arrival*

On a Sunday evening, Annie was visiting Floyd's twin sisters. She was enjoying a plate of greens, onions and cornbread, when suddenly her water broke. Annie began to feel cramping like her monthly menstrual. The twins had not had children yet, but guessed it was time for Annie to go to the hospital. Floyd was in the other room and they called to him that it was time.

The hospital called the doctor and about an hour later he was there. He told Annie that she was officially in labor, but by law, unless she or the baby was in trouble, she would have to wait the full eight-teen hours before they could administer the caesarian surgery. Gratefully for Annie, the doctor gave her a shot that allowed her to sleep throughout the labor.

When Annie awoke on May 8, 1969, a gorgeous baby girl was born. She weighed 8lbs 6oz.; had a thick afro; the cutest long eye lashes and brown eyes; round face; and her head was pretty large. She was named Whitney Ann Hightower. Annie kissed her, but couldn't hold her long. Annie was diagnosis with chronic anemia. With an extreme low red blood count and low blood pressure, the doctors couldn't understand how Annie got around as well as she did without complaining and seeking help for her condition. They predicted that Annie would remain in the hospital for ten days. During that time Annie regretted that she was unable to breast feed her baby. Annie was thankful to God that her baby was in perfect health.

After the fifth day in the hospital, Floyd approached Annie about his concerns about the medical bill and thought the baby could stay with one of their relatives until Annie got home. Annie reluctantly agreed. Her sister Claudine was in town and helped Margaret with the baby. It was difficult for Annie not being able to see her baby for five days; therefore, she concentrated on getting stronger so that she could be a good mother.

On the tenth day, Annie was released from the hospital. She didn't go home. Instead, she had Floyd take her straight to her parent's house to get her baby. When they arrived, Claudine was calming the crying baby.

"Come on and get this crying thang," Claudine said, when she saw Annie.

Annie rushed to get her baby. She thanked Claudine for helping out and held her baby close and kissed her. The baby stopped crying. Margaret and Jessie were nowhere in sight. But, two of Annie's brothers, Junior and Robert Lee, stood near-by and watched. Claudine seemed agitated.

"Why don't you take that little crying thing and your ugly husband and get out of here." Claudine shouted at Annie.

"No one here is as ugly as you and your husband," Annie said in defense.

Annie was still standing holding her baby, with about 20 stitches on her stomach, when, for the second time, in less than a month, she felt a great force across her face. Claudine had slapped Annie. Floyd charged towards Claudine, but the two brothers intervened and held Floyd from her.

"It's not worth it Floyd, let's go home," Annie shouted.

Again, Annie tried to rationalize what had happened. Claudine had a recent miscarriage; seeing the new baby might have been more than Claudine could handle. But in truth, Annie knew it was much more than that.

# CHAPTER 34

### *Adjusting*

Annie didn't have a baby shower, but her relatives and in-laws had bought a few items to help them get started with the new baby. Annie set the baby's bassinet next to her bedside. Floyd slept on the couch for a while so he could get some sleep. He couldn't stand to hear the baby cry. Sometimes he would scream, "Shut her up." This frightened Annie. Annie had heard stories about soldiers who came back from the Vietnam and Korean wars that had flash backs from baby cries. It was said that the baby cries brought attention to the enemy when they were trying to hide. So every time the baby cried Annie would jump up to quiet her or move the baby in another room.

Annie had a vertical surgical scar that ran about an inch below her navel down through her pubic hairs and held together with about 20 metal stitches. After two weeks, she had them removed and wore a panty girdle to give her support. Other than the pain and the scar there was no physical evidence that she had a baby. She gained only 25 pounds throughout the pregnancy and lost about 30 pounds by the time her stitches were removed. It was a bit difficult for her to get around and she didn't have much help. She wasn't supposed to do any

lifting for about six weeks. Floyd went to work
and washed dishes a few times. He didn't change
diapers nor feed the baby. When the baby was
about two weeks old, an elderly lady knocked
on the door. She identified herself as Alice
Waters and said she lived next door. Mrs.
Waters was about seventy-five years old and
was a retired pediatrician nurse. She told
Annie that she heard the baby crying and
wondered if Annie needed any help. Annie felt
like God had sent an angel to her.

Mrs. Walters came over almost every day
to help Annie sterilize the bottles, prepare
milk formula, and wash the cloth diaper. Annie
didn't have a washer and dryer, but until Annie
got on her feet, Mrs. Water offered to let them
use hers. She taught Annie how to make a
schedule for feeding time; how, when, and what
to feed the baby; the proper way to hold and
burp a baby, and to make a sleeping schedule.
Annie listened intensely and with Mrs. Walters
guidance, sweet baby Whitney was sleeping
through the night by the time she was two
months old.

Annie and Floyd had not gone to any church
together except for funerals and they had not
talked about religious options. Annie had
grown up as a CME and Floyd's family was
Baptist. Annie had attended other Christian
churches including Baptist. She enjoyed them

all. But, she felt that she was not yet committed or dedicated enough to any particular Christian domination. She was willing to explore and learn about others.

Mrs. Walters' practiced Seven Day Adventist, and invited Annie to service on Saturdays. Annie went to a few of the services and truly enjoyed the services, but again, she was not ready to commit. Floyd wasn't interested in church. He never made any spiritual reference to Annie that gave her an idea if he even believed in God.

Annie thought of Floyd as a generous person, but he also expected so much more from others. As months passed Annie learned a little more about the darkness she saw in Floyd, especially towards his mother. Floyd's father left his family when he was a very young boy. His father never divorced his mother, but, moved in with another woman about two miles away from their house. His father had several more children with the woman. Floyd stored a lot of anger towards his father, but when his father died, the anger was directed toward his mother. Annie was very concerned about Floyd's relation with his mother, because she believed it told a lot about him and how he treated the women in his life. She wondered why Floyd chose her.

About a week after Mrs. Waters came over to introduce herself, Floyd approached Annie and showed her the hospital bill. He told her that she needed to help pay the bill. It had only been three weeks since she gave birth and had surgery; Annie's feelings were really hurt. But, being too proud, she wouldn't let him know that she was offended.

In a couple of days Annie started the interview process. She interviewed at several businesses, but, when she told them she just had a baby, they told her to come back in a few more weeks. Floyd finally accepted the fact that no one was going to hire Annie without a medical release.

# CHAPTER 35

## *Employed*

Exactly six weeks after giving birth. Annie started working for a non-profit organization in the downtown area. She was a payroll clerk and earned a little over minimum wage. Mrs. Walters kept Whitney two or three days a week and relatives rotated on the other days. Annie enjoyed her job and the people she worked with. Floyd took Annie's check every payday. She had to ask him for money or permission to get money from the bank. He shopped for Annie's clothes that were very conservative styles.

Some of the female co-workers asked Annie to join them for lunch. Once Floyd learned of this he cooked her lunch and took it to Anna's office. It was a welcoming surprise the first time he delivered her lunch, but, it soon became embarrassing to Annie as he placed a dripping plate of food on her desk on a regular basis.

Floyd didn't want Annie to drive to work. So, he sold her car and drove her to work whenever he could. She rode the bus on days that he could not drive her.

Annie befriended another co-worker name Rena. They worked in the same department.

**168**

Annie thought Rena appeared to be a bit light headed about serious issues. Rena's boyfriend, Peanut, beat her on a regular basis. But, she didn't seem to have a major issue with it. Annie felt sorry for Rena.

When Floyd came into the office, he and Rena had private conversations that were too far a distance for Annie to hear. Annie could see them talk and laugh, but was totally unaware of their flirting.

After six months on the job another co-worker confronted Annie about a work matter and shouted at her. He was a white guy, named Bob, who had a senior level position. Annie was still a little upset when Floyd came for her. During the route home Annie shared the incident with him. Floyd made a U-turn in the road and drove all the way back to Annie's office. He rushed in with Annie in tow. Floyd knew who Bob was and as soon as Floyd saw Bob, he rushed over to him. Floyd grabbed him by his collar and lifted him against the wall. He shouted all kinds of swear words and threatened him. Annie yelled for Floyd to stop. Other employee came out of their offices and pulled Floyd off of him.

No complaints or charges were made against Floyd, but, in about a month Annie's employment there ended.

Annie learned from that experience that she had to be careful of what she said and shared with Floyd.

# CHAPTER 36

### Dates

After being fired from her job, Annie was happy to spend more time with her baby, Whitney. With pressure from Floyd, she went on other interviews. Floyd started to take Annie out on dates. The dates were limited to wrestling matches and X-Rated movies at the adult movie theatre. The activities were downtown. Annie didn't care much about the wrestling matches; wrestling and boxing were a bit too barbaric to her. Annie was just happy being out with her man.

When Annie went to the X-rated movies, she enjoyed some of them. She and Floyd would try out some of the moves when they got home. Annie loved when he lifted her and set her on his lap and entered her. He specifically liked giving Annie oral sex. Annie didn't like to give Floyd oral sex because he wasn't circumcised and when the skin on his penis was bulled back it did not feel clean to Annie. However, she would occasionally do the wifely thing. Floyd was a bit too large for Annie, but, he was able to satisfy her. During the act and in the moments of excitement and passion, Floyd always told Annie, "Your pussy is snapping." Annie guessed that was good, but, felt Floyd always wanted more than she could give.

About six months after Whitney was born, Annie experienced some vaginal itching and discharge. There was a strong odor and sex was extra painful. Annie did not complain, but, was concerned. So, Annie shared the details of her symptoms with Floyd and told him that she needed to see her OB-Gyn. Floyd insisted that she visit his doctor. He told Annie that the doctor was good and that he trusted him. So Annie once again abided. The doctor told Annie it was probably stress from after child birth and gave her a prescription for "Metronidazol". Annie followed the doctor's orders and in about three weeks the symptoms subsided.

More than a year later while putting away laundry, Annie found in Floyd's drawer a prescription bottle that was stuck in a pair of his socks. The prescription had Floyds name on it and was dated over a year prior. The bottle still had two tablets in it. The medicine was prescribed by the same doctor who prescribed medicine for her during the same period. The medicine in the bottle was called "Metronidazol".

Annie decided to do a little investigation. She called the doctor's office where she was employed while in high school and asked to speak to the nurse. Annie gave the nurse the name of the medication.

"What is the medicine used for?" Annie asked.

"It is a common medicine used for STD's, specifically, for the treatment of Trichomoniasis," the nurse told Annie.

From that moment, Annie felt no sexual obligations to her husband.

# CHAPTER 37

### *The Glass Candle*

While Annie was unemployed, she noticed Floyd drank more and he stayed away from home days at a time. After being MIA for three days, Annie sat up and waited on him. He had never been gone more than three days before so she thought she could time his return. Sure enough, Floyd entered the house late that evening. Annie had put Whitney to bed. When he entered the door, Floyd was surprised to see Annie awake and sitting in his recliner chair.

"Hi," he said.

"Hi where have you been for three days?" she asked.

"I was working undercover."

"Where are your guns?" she asked him.

"Why?" he demanded.

"How do you go to work undercover without your guns?"

Annie knew his guns were still in the bedroom drawer next to the bed. Floyd became very agitated.

"Shut up," he screamed at Annie.

"You are so gullible," he told her.

Annie remained seated with her legs up on the ottoman. Floyd picked up the large glass candle that sat on the coffee table. He threw it so hard at Annie's lower leg it ripped the skin wide open and the blood gushed out. Floyd ran to get a towel, but could not stop the bleeding. He placed Whitney in the backseat of the car; and helped Annie into the car. Floyd drove over the speed limits to the hospital emergency. He told the doctor that Annie had fallen.

While being checked in, Annie called her parents. When they arrived to the emergency, Jessie and Margaret were very upset. Annie asked her parents to take her to their home. Jessie and Floyd had a few heated words. Margaret made it known to Floyd that she knew Annie did not fall. Margaret took the baby. After Annie's leg was stitched, Jessie and Margaret took Annie and the baby home with them.

About two days later, Annie interviewed at a bank and got the position as a bookkeeper. The bank was owned by a Black organization and it was located in downtown Memphis. Annie thought about all the things that she should do to make a better life for her and her baby. She knew she would have to go back to college and find an apartment.

**175**

Annie called the apartment just to check
if Floyd was there. He didn't answer, so she
decided to go back to the house to get clothes
for her and Whitney. Annie's oldest brother
Junior was out of the Navy and back in Memphis.
He had started a job and had an apartment not
too far from her parent's home. She called him
and he agreed to take her to the house. While
Junior waited in the car, Annie let herself in
with her key and ran to the back to gather
items. She packed the car with as much as she
could, but, was fearful that Floyd would come
home.

On her way back she stopped at the
community college to check out the program
offerings. She grabbed a lot of brochures and
headed back to her parents house.

While driving, Annie and Junior had a
brief conversation.

"Mother told me to protect her when Daddy
hit her. I don't think women should be beaten,
but depending on the woman, sometimes they ask
for it," Junior told her.

Annie had never recalled her brother
given her any advice or sharing any life
wisdom. Junior's comments only confirmed to
her how cold hearted and disrespectful her
brother was towards women. She could not
respond to him. Annie loved her brother, but,

lost respect for him every time he opened his mouth.

Floyd continued to call and went by Annie's parent's house. One evening he went to the back door looking for Annie. Daisy, who was 14 years old, was in the kitchen and she let Floyd in.

"Annie is just spoiled; you need to beat her," she whispered to Floyd.

Daisy was not aware that she was over heard by other family members. Annie decided not to see or talk to Floyd at that time.

Floyd still came by, and every time he did, he and Jessie would have words. One time Jessie was holding the baby outside on the front porch, when Floyd drove up. Floyd said something that ticked Jessie off.

"Get off my property." Jessie shouted.

"That's my child and I'm not going," Floyd said.

He started to walk towards Jessie who was still holding the baby. Annie quickly approached them.

"Give me my Baby," she shouted.

She took the baby from her father.

"Leave now and I will talk with you later," she told Floyd.

Annie knew she could not continue to put this type of interruption and stress on her parents. She didn't know what Floyd was capable of and didn't want anyone to get hurt. The next day after work, Annie searched for an apartment she could afford. She saw about five apartments, but, all turned her down because of her age. She was under 21 years old and she would need a co-signer. Annie did not want to ask her parents for anything else.

Annie was on a lunch break and decided to go with some co-workers to a restaurant that was walking distance. Annie had changed her style of clothes to a more fashionable look. She wore a green suit with a short length skirt that was above her knees. As she and her co-workers step out of the bank building onto the main street, Floyd slowly drove up to Annie. Annie was surprised to see him. Floyd looked tired.

"Hello Annie, can we talk for a moment?"

Annie told her co-workers that she would catch-up with them later and got into the car. Floyd took her to another restaurant; they talked. Annie knew that if she did go back to Floyd, she could never go back to her parents.

# CHAPTER 38

### *Dance, Dance ...What*

"Hey Honey," Annie said to Floyd as he came out of the bedroom dressed in uniform and ready for work.

"Hey," Floyd replied.

"Just wanted you to know that your sister, Ruby, planned to pickup Whitney and me this afternoon. So we won't get back until late."

"Yeah, okay," he kissed Annie and left.

Annie had made a big effort to keep things calm and as normal as possible between she and Floyd. She was determined to do what she could to make their marriage work.

Once over to her twin sister in-laws' home, a couple of their cousins invited Annie to go to a club to dance. They were all church goers and none drank alcohol, so, Annie was very surprised that they wanted to go. Annie hesitated, but Ruby, Floyd's younger sister, insisted that she would watch Whitney; and indicated that they had to go to church the next morning, so the others couldn't stay out late. Annie agreed to go.

The place wasn't crowded yet because it was still early. The music was kicking and

**179**

Annie looked forward to dancing. It had been quite awhile since she danced. The ladies found a table and everyone ordered a soda. A couple people ordered chicken wings. It was 1970 and the new hits were playing: Jackson5, "I Want You Back" and "ABC"; Dianna Ross, "Ain't No Mountain High Enough"; Stevie Wonder, "Signed Sealed And Delivered"; Freda Payne, "Band of Gold". Then came the old school R&B songs: The Temptations, Marvin Gaye, The Miracles, Four Tops and more. Annie couldn't hold it any longer. She got on the floor and stayed on it.

Annie danced… and danced… and someone touched her on the shoulder. She turned around and looked straight at a police badge. She raised her eyes and there was Floyd. She was totally outdone. Floyd escorted Annie off the dance floor and out of the building. He placed her in the rear of his squad car; took her back to his sister's house; picked up Whitney; gave the baby to Annie; drove them home; let them out; opened the front door; got back into the squad car and left.

# CHAPTER 39

### Truth Surfaces

One of Floyd's older brothers passed away. Annie was very supportive and sympathetic towards Floyd. Although he handled the death well, she made herself available to him. The funeral was held at a country church and lasted over two hours. The repast was at Floyd's mother's house. Several tables were setup outside and in the house.

Floyd interacted with his relatives and got separated from Annie. She met a host of his relatives as she moved around to talk and introduced herself. Annie saw Floyd's younger brother, Andrew, sitting alone at a table outside. She walked over to the table and set down across from Andrew. They talked a while about the funeral services and what he had been doing the past year.

"Andrew, have you found an apartment yet?" Annie asked.

"I've had an apartment for over three years," he told her.

Annie was confused.

"Then why did you use Floyd's apartment to bring your girlfriends?"

Andrew was surprised and looked around to see who was near them.

"Annie, I have never used Floyd's house, and I've never taken a girl over there," he whispered.

Enough said.

# CHAPTER 40

## *Crying Baby*

Baby Whitney's crib was placed in the room beside the living room. She was a crying baby which meant that everything and anything set her off. Sometimes it was easy for Annie to calm her, but there were times it was almost impossible to satisfy her. One morning when Whitney was about eleven months old, she wanted to get out of crib. Annie was in the bathroom and couldn't get to her before Whitney started to cry.

Annie heard Floyd shout "Shut her up." Annie rushed to finish her business, but didn't get to Annie before Floyd had reached Whitney with a large black leather belt that he used to carry his guns and equipment. Annie came out in time to see Floyd raise his belt to strike the baby who stood at the foot of her crib crying. Annie made a giant leap between the belt and the baby. She felt a great pain across her arm and shoulder.

"Don't you hurt my baby," she shouted.

Floyd hit Annie a few more times with the belt.

"Didn't I tell you to keep her quiet- I have to work," he shouted back.

Annie stood firm and would not let Floyd near Whitney.

She screamed "Stop."

Floyd had never seen Annie in that form, so he stopped and walked back into the bedroom.

Whitney was screaming louder. There was so much fear in her little eyes. Annie felt like she had failed as a mother in finding security for her child. She watched Whitney while she sucked her little fingers and held tightly to her mother. Annie knew personally the feeling of security and comfort the thumb sucking brought to a child. Annie held on to Whitney until Floyd left the house. Annie sang to baby Whitney.

"Lord, build a fence all around me every day."

## CHAPTER 41

*No Education*

Little Whitney was walking and potty trained by thirteen months and she had become a bit more independent. Annie was now 20 years old and felt it was a good time to put a plan in motion to accomplish a few of her life's goals. She was determined to get a good education and had decided to major in the business field.

One weekend, Annie had pulled out some brochures that she had set aside awhile before, from the city college, to read about some of its programs for non-traditional students. She circled some ideas and wrote some phone numbers down to call. She figured she could start with two classes a semester for the first year just to adjust and then find financial aid to return full-time.

Floyd walked in from work. He played with Whitney for a moment and asked Annie what she was doing. Annie was excited about her ideas that she'd planned and was eager to share them with Floyd in hope to get some feedback on how it could work.

After telling Floyd her educational plans, without a word, Floyd walked away and went to the bedroom. He changed his clothes

and moments later Annie heard him go into the
kitchen to fix a drink. She knew something bad
was about to happen.  Annie got Whitney dressed
for bed; she read a little book to her and laid
Whitney down for the night.

Floyd was in the living room with the TV
on. Annie sat on the sofa near him, and did
not speak.  He continued to drink, but he did
not speak.  Annie decided to go to bed. She
stood up to leave.

"Where are you going?" Floyd asked her.

"To bed," she said.

"So you think you are going to college
uh?" he asked.

Annie again caught off guard, "Yes."

"I don't think so. Who do you think you
are? I don't have a college degree and you
don't need one. You will not be going to no
damn college," Floyd ordered and continued to
drink.

# CHAPTER 42
*More Babies-Not*

Annie immediately got on birth control pills after her six weeks checkup. It was very clear that they could not afford any more children at the time and she was pretty sure she didn't want anymore. Her greatest concern about having children was keeping them safe. How can she keep a child safe if she didn't feel safe?

One morning Annie got up to take the BC pill. She couldn't find the round packaged pills. She looked all over the house and when Floyd came home, he claimed he didn't know where they were. Annie knew that she would probably start spotting if she didn't soon get the pills. She felt very suspicious about her missing pills and thought Floyd knew more than he was telling.

The next day, Annie went to the Planned Parenthood to get more tablets. They gave her a three month supply. Annie put one in her purse and the remaining two she hid under the bed.

About three weeks later, Annie caught Floyd going through her purse and he had the pills in his hand.

"What are you doing? she asked.

"You don't need to take these," he demanded.

"Floyd, I don't want to get pregnant again. We just had a baby and we are struggling. Let me have the pills," pleaded Annie.

Floyd threw the pills down the toilet. Annie was upset, but knew she had two more packages under the bed. She continued to take the pills without Floyd knowledge.

# CHAPTER 43

### *Policeman Under Fire*

One evening, Floyd came home and told Annie she needed to do something for him. He was very disturb and looked desperate.

"A complaint has been filed against me by a lady who said I made her daughter get an abortion. I need you to say that you know this girl and that she told you that it wasn't true," he explained.

"How old is the girl?" Annie asked.

"What the damn difference does that makes?" Floyd yelled and then said,

"She is 14 years old."

Annie didn't have anything else to say. She felt so much pain for the little girl. She didn't want to believe she married a monster who molests (or rapes by law) little girls. But, she thought it was a possibility. Annie didn't say no to Floyd that day, but she knew in her heart if anyone ever asked her-- she would not lie.

Annie never had to lie. Somehow, the complaint was dropped, but it remained an issue with Floyd's employers and stayed in the back of Annie's mind.

## CHAPTER 44

*Nightmare*

A few weeks later, Floyd came home drunk and went straight to bed. Annie set up with Whitney until she fell asleep. Annie put on her gown; checked the doors and went to bed. Later during the night Annie was awaken by loud screams. It took her a moment to realize that it was Floyd screaming. The sound was so piercing and scary. He cried and threw his hands around. Annie got out of the bed and tried to talk to him, but was afraid to get too close to him. Then there were knocks on the door. Annie eased to the door.

"Who is it?"

"The police."

She gingerly opened the door, forgetting she only had a short gown on. She didn't want to turn the lights on because she thought it might wake the baby.

"We heard there is a disturbance here," the policeman said.

"It's my husband. I think he had a bad nightmare," Annie said.

Annie allowed the police who was holding flash lights to go to the bedroom. Once they were in the bedroom they talked to Floyd;

who never got out of the bed, but assured the officers that he was okay. They knew Floyd from the force and they were satisfied with what he said, so the officers left.

Annie was so thankful that the baby slept through the entire incident. Floyd never talked to Annie about what had happen. She thought it had something to do with posttraumatic stress disorder (PTSD) that some ex-soldiers suffered from.

The following month, Floyd moved the family into another apartment. He never explained why. The new place was located on the second floor of a large complex. It was a down grade, but Annie did not complain.

One day at the new apartment, Annie answered the door to two ladies who were Jehovah Witnesses. She had nothing to do and Whitney was napping, so she let them in the apartment. They shared some brochures with Annie and talked about the content. Annie enjoyed their company. They invited her to their Hall and Annie accepted.

The first time Annie went to the Hall, one of the ladies named Terri, drove her and Whitney there. Annie enjoyed the people and the services and went back a few more times. Annie and Terri became close friends. Terri offered to pierce Annie's ears. Annie was excited that she would be able to wear earrings all the time.

One day while Floyd was at work, Terri arrived at the apartment. As instructed, Annie put some ice cubes in a bowl for Terri. A chair was placed next to the kitchen sink where Annie sat. Once Terri placed the supplies, (a towel, two needles that had been double threaded, alcohol and peroxide) on the counter, she was ready to start.  Terri cleaned both ears thoroughly with alcohol. Treating one ear at a time, Terri took two pieces of the ice cubes and placed one in front of the ear lobe and one in back of the ear lobe; she held the ice cubes in place until the lobe was practically frozen. She then picked up the needle and pierced it in the center of the lobe all the way through to the other side; cleaned it with peroxide; cut the needle from the thread; tied the thread to make a loop; clean the ear again, and it was all done. She showed Annie how to take care of her ears. Annie claimed that other than the initial coldness from the ice cubes, she didn't feel anything.

Terri continued to come over to meet with Annie for bible study. Annie enjoyed the meetings, but still was not ready to commit to joining because to her there were some contradictions in its practices.

The following Sunday, Annie went to church without Whitney. The baby was still at Floyd's sister's house and had spent the night while Annie and Floyd went to a wrestling match. Annie had arranged to get Whitney after church.

Annie rode with Terri to the hall. About one half hour into the service Floyd arrived. He sat next to Annie.

"Let's go."

"Is everything okay?" Annie asked.

Floyd grabbed Annie's arm and guided her to the exit door.

Once outside Annie asked Floyd,    "What is going on?"

"I don't want you coming here anymore." Floyd shoved Annie towards the car.

"Now get in the car," he demanded.

Terri had followed them outside to see if anything was wrong.

"Annie, are you leaving?" she asked.

"You cannot come to my house anymore," Floyd interrupted.

"Terri I will call you later," Annie said.

"No you want. Now get in," Floyd said as he pushed Annie into the car.

Floyd slammed the car door; walked around to the driver's door; got in and drove away.

# CHAPTER 45
## *Gullible*

It was a very cold day in February 1971. Floyd was gathering tax documents to submit to the tax preparer. Annie handed him her W2 form that included only eight months of work at the Bank. Annie was forced to resign from her job, because of Floyd, who again came on her job and caused problems. The bank had zero tolerance with his unannounced appearances and rude attitude towards some of the men who worked there. Annie resigned to avoid being fired. Annie was now unemployed, but was aware that she was turning 21 years old within weeks and knew she had more options.

When Floyd completed the income tax return, he hid the return from Annie. She never thought to ask Floyd about it.

One night during the following month, Floyd came home drunk. He was agitated and looking for a fight. Annie thought he was handling Whitney a little too rough and took her away from him. Floyd got upset and slapped Annie across her face. Annie, with Whitney in her arms, ran into the bedroom and she locked the bedroom door. Floyd yelled:

"You are a gullible bitch. Don't even think about leaving me. I will kill you first. Your parents will never see the baby

**195**

again. No one will want you anyway with a
baby. You can't even have a baby the normal
way-- paying all that money just to have a
baby."

Floyd went on and on.

"So gullible, you think you got pregnant
by accident - well your mother should have
told you about the rhythm method. Don't have
to be Catholic to know that. Shoot- anybody
can count to 14. You can't even hold a
whiskey sour-- So damn gullible."

Floyd finally stopped talking. Annie had
locked the bedroom door and sealed it off with
a chair. She knew her marriage was over. She
was beyond hurt and couldn't think. Annie knew
then that her entire relationship and marriage
to Floyd was based on deceit and manipulation.

"Where is the love?" she thought. Annie
clearly saw that Floyd wanted her isolated from
her family, the world and from God so that he
could have total control over her. Annie held
Whitney tightly and prayed:

"Lord, build a fence all around me every
day."

About two week later, while Floyd was at
work, Annie checked the mailbox. Inside was a
federal income tax refund letter. She
immediately ripped it open, and there was a

check for $275. Annie hid the check between a set of encyclopedias and prayed for a sign to make her move.

*"Change is what life is about. As we evolve, options are presented to some; while others see only oppression, and no other options are available except to accept oppression --for a moment."*

# CHAPTER 46

*Time To Go*

"There will be peace in the valley for me, some day." The song was playing on the radio.

It was a beautiful sunny spring day in April 1971 and Margaret was dressing to attend her father's funeral. Her mother, Grandma McGwin, was in the girl's room also preparing. They were singing along with the song on the radio.

Grandpapa Matthew M. McGwin died at age 81. He had been ill for a while and stayed in a convalescent home. Margaret truly loved her parents and tried to do the best she could for them. Although, this was a very sad occasion, Margaret and Jessie always enjoyed being with the McGwin family.

Annie and her siblings loved when their mother's sisters and brothers visited their home. When the McGwins got together everyone knew that there was going to be a spectacular event. Margaret and four of her siblings would get together and belt some old time spiritual and gospel songs. That day they sang, "Trouble of the World", "Amazing Grace", and "Trust in God". They had various ranges and when the youngest sister (Aunt Olivia) hit that high

"C", and the brothers harmonized, it sent chills down everybody's spine. Annie wished that she and her siblings could be as loving as her aunts and uncles appeared to be.

This was the largest family gathering ever held. The McGwin family had grown to eleven siblings; fifty five grandchildren and many great and great-greats. Papa McGwin funeral was well attended. Nine of the eleven siblings were still living during the time of the funeral; but there was representation from all eleven siblings. Family came from the USA's west coast to the east coast. Several cousins had met for the first time. Annie was so excited to meet her cousins from the San Francisco Bay Area; Los Angeles; New Jersey; and Chicago. After the funeral, Annie joined some of them and went house hopping from one cousin to another. Little Whitney was passed around from cousin to cousin and she didn't seem to be bothered by it.

Annie did not have a key to their apartment. She made a couple of calls to the house, but there was no answer. It was about midnight and little Whitney was asleep at Annie's parent's home. Annie was still with her cousins at one of the local cousin's home. She made one more attempt in vain to call Floyd. So, Annie continued to enjoy her cousins. Her cousins suggested that she spend the night and they would give her a lift home in the morning.    Annie was so tried and sleepy, she agreed.

Annie arrived at her apartment the next morning about 10 o'clock. She didn't see Floyd's car, but she knocked on the door anyway. After a couple of times, the next door neighbor came out of her apartment.

"Are you Annie, she asked.

"Yes," Annie said.

"Well your husband is on the phone. I have a key for you."

Annie walked into the lady's apartment and picked up the phone.

"Hello."

"Where have you been?" Floyd shouted.

"At my cousins; I don't have a key; I called you," Annie whispered.

"You are dead; when I get home, I will kill you!"

Annie gave the phone back to the lady and thanked her. She took the key and left.

Annie, let herself into the apartment and immediately called her mother.

"Hi Mother, how are you?"

"I'm fine and you?" Margaret replied.

"Well, Floyd said he's going to kill me when he gets home."

"Leave now --come home baby, Whitney is with me. I will send someone to get you!"

An hour later a long-time family friend who lived on the next street drove up in a large Ford. Annie loaded the car and did not forget to take the income tax check she had hidden between the encyclopedias. Annie knew that there was no going back or looking back. It was time to go.

Margaret had a younger sister who was about the same age as Annie when her husband shot and killed her over a jealous rage. So Margaret did not hesitate to do what she could to protect her daughter. Since her mother, Grandma McGwin, and her brother, Uncle Shooey had not yet left Memphis; Margaret decided to talk with them about Annie's dire situation. They readily suggested that Annie come to stay with them in St. Louis until she gets on her feet.

When Annie learned about her grandmother's and uncle's invitation, she was so grateful. But, she felt she needed to handle a few legal matters before she left Memphis.

Annie found and met with an attorney to handle the divorce and child custody matter.

Annie gave the attorney $100 to get started and promised she would have the remaining soon.

It took Annie a few days to leave Memphis. Floyd came over once, but Jessie made a firm statement to him that he was to never come on his property again. Annie did not speak with Floyd.

Annie packed two large suitcases. With 23 month old Whitney in her arms, they boarded the Greyhound bus headed to St. Louis, Mo.

Jessie and Margaret were so relieved when Annie left; as they waved goodbye to them, they knew their daughter would be safer out of Memphis.

# CHAPTER 47

### *ST. LOUIS*

Rev. George W. McGwin, Uncle Shooey, was a pastor of a CME church in St. Louis. He had served as pastor for several CME churches throughout the USA. His mother, Elizabeth M. Green McGwin also moved with him. They had lived in the St. Louis church's parish for about three years. Uncle Shooey never married and had no children. He was of small statue; stood about 5'6"; with reddish auburn hair; golden complexion with lots of freckles. He loved to laugh and tell jokes; when he laughed it was contagious- everyone laughed with him. He sang like an angel. He attended the same high school Annie attended, but before she was born.

Grandma McGwin was very proper and strict. It was difficult for Annie to imagine a very petite woman had given birth to 19 children; 4 died after birth; 4 died as toddlers; and eleven lived to be adults. Grandma McGwin stood about 5"1'. Her family mixed heritage of Native American and African gave her a beautiful smooth complexion that gave a golden glow. Annie had inherited her thin lips and square chin from her grandmother. Grandma was so proper and had no tolerance for disrespect and disruptive children. She went to church on a regular basis. She sang and played the piano.

Annie's mother, Margaret, was a very little girl when Grandma McGwin taught her how to sew. During the time when Grandma lived in Memphis, she and Margaret would get together to make church hats. The hats were different colors and made with different types of fabric with beautiful handmade flowers attached. They sold them to various church members to earn income. Sometimes they would make suits to match the hats or vice versa. What they didn't sell they wore.

Grandma McGwin had been estranged from her husband, Papa McGwin, for many years. For several years, she moved around from state to state with her son George, Uncle Shooey, who had been the pastor of several CME churches. Grandma McGwin accommodated Uncle Shooey's needs; cooked his food; washed and pressed his clothes and kept a clean house. Sometimes, she sang in the choir and played the piano during services.

The Christian Methodist Episcopal Church was located off a main street; in a clean and peaceful neighborhood. A small grocery store was located directly across from the church. The church parish was a two-story house with four bedrooms and a basement. All of the bedrooms were on the upper floor. Annie and Whitney were given the rear bedroom. It was a nice large room with a full size bed; dresser with mirror and chest-drawers. It had two large windows with a view of the back yard. Annie was so grateful to have the space and to start a new life.

# CHAPTER 48

## *New Job*

Annie settled in and immediately started to look for a job. Within a week she found employment with a nonprofit organiza-tion that helped black people get an education and provided skills training. She was so excited about her new position as a bookkeeper. Grandma McGwin volunteered to watch Whitney until a child care facility was available.

Annie was well received by her co-workers and she learned to master her duties in a short time. During that time, she befriended a couple of ladies who showed her around St. Louis for places to shop and buy discount food and clothes. They also helped Annie find a childcare center.

It was still summer time and there were some hot days. Annie didn't like to eat a lot of food when it was hot. But, she made sure that she ate a hardy lunch and when she went home she would refuse dinner. After a few refusals, Uncle Shooey was a bit offended and insisted that Annie joined him and Grandma for dinner. Annie apologized and abided. Grandma's food was very good, but it was too heavy for Annie stomach, especially after 6 p.m. She ate a little food; then cleared the table and washed the dishes. Annie did enjoy spending time with her family.

Annie tried to help Grandma as much as she could. At seventy three years old Grandma got around pretty well. The laundry room was in the basement and her bedroom was upstairs so she climbed the stairs a lot.

Annie went to the church a few Sunday. Since Annie grew up as CME, she knew the order of worship.  Uncle Shooey always preached a great message. He, Grandma and the choir always sang with such praise and inspiration.

A few times Annie went out to a club with her friends and didn't get home until about 1 a.m.  She did not have a door key; therefore, she woke up Uncle Shooey to let her in. Instead of giving her a key, he placed a midnight curfew.  Annie abided.

Annie began to save her money so that she would be able to buy a car and make a deposit on an apartment.

About two months after she left Memphis, Annie was upstairs in her bedroom reading and Whitney was with Grandma in her bedroom coloring her books, when the door bell rang. Annie's bedroom door was opened, but she didn't pay much attention to the door bell, because Uncle Shooey periodically had visitors.  It was a moment later when Annie heard footsteps coming up the stairs. She still thought it was Uncle Shooey. Then she heard more than one set of footsteps. She paused from reading; just as she got up from the bed, Floyd was standing in her room. Uncle Shooey was in the doorway. Annie stood up and stepped back.

"What are you doing here?"

Floyd walked towards Annie.

"I'm here to take you home," he said.

"I'm not going anywhere with you, Annie yelled.

"Oh yes you are!" Floyd pulled out a set of handcuffs.

The bed was blocking the exit from Annie so she jumped on the bed to run across it. Floyd caught her and knocked her to the bed. He grabbed her arms to the back of her.

"No one every leaves me," he shouted.

Just as Floyd tried to put the handcuffs on Annie, Uncle Shooey leaped between them and pushed Floyd away from Annie.

"Let her go. What are you doing?" shouted Uncle Shooey.

Annie got up and ran to Grandma's room where Whitney was still playing. She locked the door. Annie could hear Uncle Shooey shouting at Floyd.

"Get out of my house- What are you going to do- arrest her and take her back to Memphis? Get out before I call the police."

Annie heard footsteps going down the steps and then the door opened and closed. She eased out of Grandma's room and looked down the stairs. Uncle Shooey walked back up to the top of the stairs and stopped.

He laughed, "That is a crazy man-- handcuff you?" He laughed again and went back down stairs.

Annie gave her uncle a weak smile to let him know she was okay, but she knew it was a serious matter and that Floyd was not finished. She knew once again she would have to find safety. It would be years before Annie learned that her younger evil sister, Daisy, who stole her hard earned money, who told Floyd to beat her, and then, told him where to find her.

The next day she called her sister Claudine. She knew Claudine didn't like her, but Annie felt confident she would help her. Claudine loved children and would do anything to protect them.

On a Saturday morning, Annie packed up everything that she and Whitney owned; then once again mounted the Greyhound headed to Gary, Indiana. Claudine had agreed to keep Whitney until Annie found suitable housing.

**209**

When Annie returned to St. Louis, she moved in with a friend named Valencia. Annie met Valencia through a co-worker at a party. They realized that they had a few things in common and hit it off right away. Valencia was a single parent with one daughter about six years old. She had been divorced for several years. Valencia lived in a very nice two bedroom apartment. Annie was so elated that a person who she just met was so kind and trusting to let a somewhat stranger in her home. She was determined to earn that trust.

Annie slept on the sofa bed in the living room that was very comfortable. Valencia was delightful; she immediately made Annie feel at home and gave her a key to the apartment. Valencia was attractive; a fast talker; and she loved to laugh. She was about 5 feet 2 inches tall; with full curves; wore her hair cut short; she had the most beautiful golden complexion; and the brightest smile. Her daughter Lena was so cute and well behaved. Lena enjoyed reading and playing games. Valencia was down-to-earth and smart; she held a management position with a national organization.

Annie took the bus to work, but when possible, Valencia gave her a lift. Valencia showed Annie the best shopping places around town and they went out to a few night clubs.

Valencia was a great dancer and Annie tried to emulate some of her moves. She and Valencia soon developed a strong sisterhood.

Annie made a down payment on a brand new 1971 Toyota Corolla. It had standard shift, a golden color, and no air condition. She didn't mind. It was so wonderful for Annie to have the freedom to drive when and where she wanted to. No more Greyhound buses.

A few weeks later, Annie moved into her first apartment. It was a very nice two bedroom apartment that was location off a main highway. The apartment was part of a quarto-flex building. The landlord lived in the lower east apartment and Annie's apartment was the upper west. They were a married couple (David and Sylvia) with an infant baby girl (Nichole). Sylvia offered to keep Whitney when she returned from Indiana for a lower fee than the day care center. Having a sitter so close was another blessing to Annie. She didn't have to take Whitney out into extreme weather.

Whitney had been gone for almost three months. It had been difficult for Annie not to have her baby with her. Annie loaded up her new car and drove to Gary to get Whitney. The sight of Whitney's bright eyes was so heartwarming to Annie. She held on to Whitney and didn't want to let her go. Her baby was safe and healthy. Whitney had been fishing with her Uncle and loved it. Claudine had bought her a few toys and outfits. The visit was very pleasant; Annie thought no matter how much the words "thank you" came out of her mouth, Claudine and her husband didn't truly understand the impact their graciousness had on her life.

After returning to St. Louis, Whitney adjusted pretty well to the new environment. There had been so much change in her little life over the last six months. Annie looked forward to settling down.

# CHAPTER 49

*Family Lost*

Things had been going very well for Annie on the job. She had also applied at a local community college to begin classes in the upcoming spring semester. Thanksgiving was near and Annie looked forward to spending the holiday with her grandmother and uncle.

Early Tuesday morning before Thanksgiving, the phone awakened Annie. It was Uncle Shooey who called to inform Annie that Grandma was in the hospital; she had suffered a stroke. Annie was in shock and didn't know how to handle the information. Uncle Shooey let Annie know that Grandma was asleep, but to come when she could. It was only moments before the alarm would sound to get up for work. So, she turned off the alarm and got up. She prepared breakfast for Whitney and then got dressed. After dropping off Whitney at the sitter, Annie went by the office to let them know she was going to the hospital.

When Annie arrived Grandma wasn't asleep, but was heavily medicated. Annie talked to her, but wasn't sure if Grandma understood her. She stayed around until Grandma fell asleep. She went by the office for a couple of hours to complete a few assignments and then returned

**213**

to the hospital. Grandma McGwin seemed to be
in and out of consciousness. Annie was certain
that Grandma McGwin smiled at her and Annie
held her hands. It was close to the end of
visiting hours when Grandma fell asleep. Annie
kissed her and told her that she would be back
the next day.

The next morning Uncle Shooey called
Annie to tell her Grandma McGwin had passed
away and that he would call the family.

The first person Annie thought about was
her mother. Margaret had lost her father and
mother within eight months. Annie wanted to
be with her mother. It was the day before
Thanksgiving and she imagined what her mother
was doing and what she had planned for the
holiday.

Annie took a few days off from work to
return to Memphis for Grandma McGwin's
funeral. It was a beautiful service and a very
large turnout. Grandma was buried next to
Grandpa. Annie was happy to be with her family,
especially to see her mother and father again.
Jessie was so thrilled to see Annie and
Whitney. He kissed Whitney and held her for a
while.

During her visit in Memphis, Annie
decided to meet with her attorney to pay the
remaining fee and to get the divorce started.

He told Annie it would take about six months to get a hearing; this allowed time for possible reconciliation. He also let her know she would need witnesses for the alleged physical and emotional abuse. Annie thought it was a stupid law, but would deal with it when the time came.

One of Floyd's twin sisters called Annie to give her condolences and pleaded with Annie to bring Whitney by her home. They assured Annie that she would be safe. Annie with her cousin, Charles, took Whitney to see them. When Annie arrived the twins had a few relatives there just in case Floyd showed up. They had not seen Whitney for more than 8 months and were thrilled to be able to spend time with her. After about an hour later, and just as Annie prepared to leave, Floyd showed up. Annie believed the twins when they told her that they did not know he was coming over. Floyd had always dropped in unannounced by anyone's house. Floyd played with Whitney for a moment; she didn't seem to be too attached. Annie told him that she had to go. Several of Floyd's relatives walked with Annie, Charles, and Whitney to her car. Floyd noticed Annie's new car.

"Is this your car?"

"Yes," Annie said.

Floyd placed Whitney in the backseat. Annie noticed him checking out her car. Charles got inside the car.

Floyd's car was blocking Annie's car at the end of the drive way. Annie looked back at his car and noticed someone was sitting inside the car. One person asked Floyd who was in his car. He didn't respond, but the woman inside the car rolled down the window. Annie recognized her; it was her former co-worker, Rena. It had been revealed to Annie that Floyd and Rena had been in a relationship before Annie separated from him.

"Hi Annie. Why don't you let Floyd keep Whitney for the night?"

Annie became really annoyed when Rena opened her month to address her; she ignored Rena's comments.

"Floyd please move your car, we have to go now," Annie insisted.

Floyd got inside his car and moved it. Annie backed out of the driveway, waved goodbye to her in-laws, and drove away.

# CHAPTER 50

*Back To St. Louis*

As happy as Annie was to see her parents she was happier being back in her own apartment and at work. Annie was relieved that Whitney was again on a regular routine and seemed to be doing well.

The following January Annie enrolled in two classes; each met once a week. It was an adjustment, but she soon got a handle on it. There wasn't much time for a social life and Annie didn't want to meet anyone until her divorce was final. Valencia did try to setup several dates for her, but Annie declined.

It was May 8$^{th}$, Whitney's third birthday. The landlord, Sylvia had baked some cup-cakes and Annie bought ice-cream and made sandwiches. Sylvia's daughter and one other little girl were present. Annie painted her face and dressed as a clown with stuffed padding around her waist to give a jolly look.

Annie played music, dance around, and passed out little gifts. Everyone sang "Happy Birthday" to Whitney; she giggled and had so much fun. As she opened her presents, Whitney would squeal from delight until she opened the last one. She lifted the mechanical toy elephant from the box and set it on the floor.

**217**

Annie wound it up and placed it on the floor.
The elephant stood up on it rear legs and made
a weird sound. Whitney screamed. Annie turned
it off and Whitney calmed down.

Annie waited several days to try the toy
again, but Whitney screamed again. So, Annie
gave the cute little elephant away.

One evening a few days after Whitney's
birthday, Annie took her to a local grocery
store to pick up a few items. Whitney grabbed
a piece of candy from a shelf, but Annie had
never bought candy for Whitney and didn't allow
her to have it. Whitney fell out on the floor,
screamed to the top of her voice. Annie was
very surprised by this, so she walked away.
Annie kept walking.

"Ma'am don't you forget your child." The
store clerk said to Annie.

"I don't know that little girl; my child
would not act that way," Annie replied in a
loud voice.

Annie kept walking out of the store.
Within second, Annie heard Whitney running
behind her.

"Mommie, Mommie, it's me, I yo chil."

Whitney never had another public temper-
tantrum. Instead, she would go into her room
and shut the door to express herself.

# CHAPTER 51

*Divorce Hearing*

It was early summer time; rain was predicted in Memphis, and it wasn't too hot. Annie carried her purse and an umbrella as she and her mother, Margaret, entered the courthouse. They took the elevator to the 4th floor; where Annie's attorney, Sam Taylor, was waiting. Standing beside him was Annie's friend, Terri. Annie hugged Terri and thanked her for coming. Margaret and Terri had agreed to be the witnesses for the divorce hearing.

The procedures began with the swearing in. Annie stated her case and the defense attorney questioned her. Annie held her own and did well. Her mother was next. Annie's eyes filled with tears when she heard her mother testify.

"Annie was a happy girl before she got married; there wasn't much smiles soon after," Margaret told the judge.

The last witness, Terri, was called to testify. She recalled details that Annie had forgotten. Terri was confident and articulate. She did very well.

Floyd lied throughout his statements and often contradicted himself. He stated Annie beat him with a chain and kicked him. But,

**219**

the Judge saw through it all and granted Annie a divorce on grounds of emotional and physical abuse. She received full custody of Whitney and Floyd was ordered to pay $90 a month for child support.

Annie thanked her attorney, her friend Terri and her mother for all they had done. When the attorney excused himself, Annie offered to take Terri and Margaret out for a snack. Terri declined because she had made other plans. Annie took her mother out to lunch. Although Margaret did not say it, Annie knew her mother was relieved and happy for her.

When Annie got back to her parent's house, she received a phone call. It was Floyd's girlfriend, Rena.

"Annie. Why are you making Floyd pay $90 a month? That's not fair, you know he will take care of his child," she said.

Annie hung up on her. Rena had been sucked into doing Floyd's dirty deeds. The phone rang again. It was Floyd.

"If you think you are going to get any money from me- you better think again, I'm not sending you a damn penny --and remember I know where you and "your" parents live, so don't even try... things can happen." Floyd hung up.

Annie called the police and reported the threats. A police officer came out to her parent's house to interview Annie. The officer was Floyd's co-worker. After Annie told him what both Floyd and Rena had said to her, the only statement the policeman repeated was:

"He has to pay you $90 a month?!!"

Annie knew then she was on her own. She had to be self-reliant and responsible for both her and her baby. She couldn't risk the chance of anything terrible happening to her parents or to her.

# CHAPTER 52

### A Free Woman

Annie returned to St. Louis a single woman. She felt free and saw herself and the world through different eyes. Annie went to work and remained in college. She enjoyed fun outings with Whitney at the park, zoo, and amusement parks.

Valencia invited Annie and Whitney over to her house for dinner. Annie got Whitney ready, picked up a bottle of ginger ale, and headed to Valencia's place. Whitney went into the bedroom with Lena to play games.

Valencia had made a beautiful vegetable salad, salmon and rice pilaf. Her table setting reminded Annie of her mother's china, silverware, water and wine classes on a lovely table cloth.

The kids joined Valencia and Annie for dinner. When they were done, Annie and Lena helped clear the table and placed the dishes in the dish washer. Annie was relieved that there was a mechanical dish washer, since she was usually the human one.

The kids went back to doing their thing in the bedroom. Valencia played a little soft music and poured herself a glass of wine. Annie fixed a glass of ginger ale. Valencia congratulated Annie on her divorce.

"Girrrl you got to start dating. You are still young and pretty-- You need to enjoy life," Valencia rationalized.

"Yeah I guess, but it will happen when it happens," Annie said.

"Well I know this guy who is perfect for you."

"No one is perfect," Annie interrupted.

"Yeah I know, but he seems ideal for you... There will be a card party next weekend at a friend's house - He'll be there and you can check him out... I know you like playing cards," Valencia insisted.

"I need to watch my spending; I don't have the money for a sitter," Annie replied.

"Don't you worry I will take care of that- Whitney can come here with my sitter and you can spend the night too," pressed Valencia.

"Give me time to think about it," Annie said.

## CHAPTER 53

*First Date*

Annie attended the card party, but didn't feel the connection with the friend Valencia wanted her to hookup with. One weekend Annie was shopping at a grocery store with Whitney. A young man walked up to her and introduced himself as Kenneth Foster. He told Annie that they had met a couple of months before at a community meeting held by the organization she worked for. With everything on her mind during that time Annie didn't remember him, but did not say so. She shook his hand and introduced herself. He insisted that she call him Kenny. He was very attractive; mid 20's; about 6'2"; dark brown skin; a short length dark brown and well groomed afro; short beard; muscular built; and small waist. Kenny wore afro centric attire.

Are you married," Kenny asked Annie.

"No, recent divorced."

"That cute little girl must be yours."

Whitney was busy looking at some books in the children's section.

"Thank you.    Yes she is. Her name is Whitney."

"There are some community activities coming up that you and Whitney might enjoy." He wrote his phone number down on a piece of paper.

"Here is my number. May I have your phone number?

Annie said her phone number as he wrote it down.

A couple of days later, Kenny called Annie and asked her out. She accepted.

The first date was dinner and a movie. Kenny was a gentleman and very frugal. Annie thought that was good, because he had a plan. Kenny had his own computer and soft-ware business. He had never been married, but wanted to marry and to have a few children. Annie thought of him as very traditional. He wanted to buy a home and invest in other real-estate.

Annie saw a very kind and gentle soul in Kenny and truly enjoyed his company. They went out on a few more dates including a community play. Kenny also took Annie and Whitney to the zoo and park. Kenny loved children and Annie was pleased as to how patient and gentle he was with Whitney.

One evening after a date, Kenny invited Annie to his place. Kenny turned down the light and play soft music. He poured Annie a glass of seven up soda with a lime twist and one for himself. Kenny set on the sofa next to Annie. They talked about the day, politics, and he showed Annie some family photos; they laughed and told stories.

Kenny reached over to Annie and kissed her. She kissed him back. She loved his scent, it was fresh and intoxicating. He kissed her hard and held her tighter.

It had been a while for Annie and she wasn't sure what to do. So she did nothing, but relaxed and let Kenny take control. He took off her top and kissed her nipples and stomach. Annie laid down quietly on the sofa. Kenny removed her pants and shoes and spread her legs. He kissed her on her thighs and between her legs, and moved upward to lick her. Annie moaned as he continued to lick harder and harder. Annie cried out; she thought that she would lose her mind, he sucked a little harder; Annie screamed, "Don't stop." Kenny continued until Annie reached a climax. Then he entered her. He moved his body with a gentle force. Annie grabbed his butt and pulled him closer to her. She moaned. He moaned. Their bodies moved together in harmony. They kissed and turned on their side; still holding each other tightly. They continued until Annie reached a climax again and Kenny joined her.

Annie was grateful that Kenny took the initiative to use a condom.

Annie and Kenny continued to see one another and made beautiful love until they had "the talk". Kenny wanted more in the relationship and was prepared to make a commitment. He wanted marriage and children. Annie was far left of that, she had recently divorced; hadn't had a chance to know the person she was; she wanted a career; and she probably didn't want any more children.

Annie and Kenny remained friends without benefits. Although she missed his loving, Annie didn't want to mislead him into thinking there was a future together.

# CHAPTER 54

### Comfort

Annie knew a lot about the comfort of thumb sucking. She also knew about the cruel teasing done by others to the thumb sucker. Besides the teasing, Annie was aware of the long-term defects to the teeth and gums. She would do anything within her power to ease any possible humiliation imposed on her daughter. Since the home environment seemed calm and Whitney was sucking her thumb mostly when she was sleepy or sleeping, Annie thought the shoe lace she used for herself would be too extreme for Whitney. So, she devised a different method.

One night, Annie let Whitney sleep with her. Once Whitney fell asleep with her thumb in her mouth, Annie simply pulled it out. That was it. Annie did that all through the night for three nights straight. Whitney never sucked her thumb again.

Annie knew that there were some things that could be changed, while there were many things that couldn't be changed.

When Annie took Whitney for her twelve month check up, the pediatrician had noticed that Whitney's legs were turned inward that caused her knees to rub against one another.

He highly recommended that Annie invest in some special shoes for at least two years to straighten out her legs.

Prior to the doctor's appointment, Annie's sister, Samantha, had brought Whitney's legs to her attention, but in a tensing manner. Annie personally knew how teasing affects a child confidence and well-being. But, Annie wasn't aware then that there was a fix for Whitney's legs. She was relieved to hear the doctor say that Whitney's legs could be straightened. Annie bought the shoes; she didn't care how much they cost and how long it took.

The prescribed shoes worked; by the age of three years old, there was no evidence that Whitney's legs were any different than the perfect legs that existed.

Whitney inherited both her mother's and father's big heads. Annie was aware that she couldn't do anything about the teasing. Since Annie had a big head too; she learned to deal with it; and Whitney would as well.

"A big head - A big brain. That's all good," was Annie's thoughts on that subject.

## CHAPTER 55

### Washington, DC

The nonprofit organization Annie worked for had annual national conventions. That year, it was held in Washington, DC for four days. Annie had worked hard with her supervisor to prepare needed reports for special presentations. She had never been to DC and looked forward to going.

Annie traveled with four other co-workers. She shared a room with a young lady named Kelly, who worked in the education division. Once at the convention, Annie met many people from all over the United States. In addition, to the planned meetings, there were other activities scheduled. Annie didn't sleep much; she tried to attend every meeting and activity. She toured many of the district's attractions; the capital, white house, the Monument, Lincoln and Jackson Memorials, and more.

On the night of the closing banquet, Annie dressed eloquently. She wore a form fitting black dress with a split on one side of the dress; she braided her hair and loosened the braids to give a full curly stylish look; and wore large hoop silver earrings. After the dinner ended, popular music was played. Annie hoped someone would ask her to dance. Instead, a man approached her in his forties, about 5'6", heavy built and receding hairline. He removed his glasses and he introduced himself.

"Hi, I'm Ralph Carter, the Executive Director of the San Francisco Division."

Annie extended her hands to shake his.

"Hi, I'm Annie Hightower, from St. Louis."

"What do you do there?" he asked.

"I'm a bookkeeper."

"Have you ever been to California?"

"No. I have not; but I do have an aunt and dozens of cousins in the San Francisco Bay Area and Los Angeles areas.

He gave Annie his business card.

"Well contact me for a job opportunity in accounting, if you decide to join your relatives in the area."

"Thank you very much. I will remember that."

Annie and one of her co-workers were given an invitation to a party on the same evening. It was in the suite of a well known civil rights leader. Annie was flattered that she was invited and accepted. When she and her co-worker entered the suite, there were about ten people there. The guy who invited Annie introduced her to the Host. Annie had read a lot about the civil rights movement and the well known Host; and she had participated in several events. Annie was so honored to speak with him and was talking so much, she didn't notice that everyone else had left and she was alone with him.

"Not again- how did I fall for this," Annie thought.

Annie stopped talking and stared at the host.

"You really don't want to be here, do you?" he asked Annie.

She felt relieved.

"No. It was a pleasure meeting you," she said to him; she stood and left the room.

Annie went downstairs where her co-workers and the guy who had invited her were drinking and listening to music. They were surprised to see Annie. She gave them a look that clearly stated that she did not appreciate the "setup".

Annie danced, "free-style" once that evening, and then turned in for the night.

# CHAPTER 56

### *Hot Pants*

One evening Annie got dressed in her hot pants and knee high fitted boots; the top was short with her midriff shown; she tied a headband through her long pressed hair and put on a pair of large hoop earrings. Annie was ready to dance. Valencia invited her to go to a club that was having a contest for "Miss Hot Pants". That sounded like fun to Annie; all she wanted to do was dance.

The club was full when they arrived. There were black lights and flashing colored dance floor lighting. A large glittering disco light hung over the dance floor.

Ladies were dressed in hot pants, mini-skirts, knee high boots, Mary Jane shoes, hip-huggers, and bell bottoms. The men had their afros together and wore polyester prints, leisure suits, and platform and pimp shoes.

The DJ played some of the latest music such as Al Green, "Let's stay together" and "I'm still in love with you"; Jean Knight, "Mr. Big Stuff"; The Temptations, "Papa was a Rollin' Stone"; Jackson5, "Never Can Say Goodbye"; James Taylor, "You've got a friend"; The Staple Singers, "I'll take you there"; The Stylistics, "Betcha By Golly, Wow" and "You are everything". Some "oldie-but-goodies" were also played.

People were on the floor mostly dancing freestyle disco. But, the hustle line dance had recently come out and a lot of people got on the floor. They also danced the "bump".

The DJ announced that it was time for the Miss Hot Pants contest. He asked all the ladies who wore hot pants to go on the dance floor. Annie didn't go.

"What are you waiting for – you better git up there girl- you got this! Now go!" Valencia told Annie.

Annie still didn't go. The DJ played, The Chi-Lites, "Have you seen her". There were about fifteen ladies on the floor. Annie thought it was all in fun, so she decided to go. As each contestant strutted across the floor, the guests applauded for the best Miss Hot Pants. Unexpectedly, Annie became "Miss Hot Pants " of 1972. The DJ placed a banner over her shoulder and photos were taken. A few days later Annie saw her photo in a local newspaper.

## CHAPTER 57

*Revelation*

That evening, after the contest was over, a very attractive young man came up to Annie; he smiled and introduced himself as Dmitri. Annie, feeling a bit more confident, smiled back. They talked a few minutes; they exchanged phone numbers and Annie told him she had to leave.

About a week later Dmitri called Annie. He apologized for taking so long to call, but he had been working on closing a business deal. Annie had thought a lot about Dmitri and hoped he would call. They made a date for the following weekend.

Dmitri was about 5'11 with a smooth brown complexion; slim built with a narrow waistline. He had brown eyes with long eyelashes; wore a medium length afro that was well maintained. He dressed in medium height platforms that raised his height to about 6'2". He was articulate and charming.

Annie enjoyed the first outing with Dmitri. He took her to a very nice restaurant and wanted to talk about her.

"You are a very lovely lady, Annie. We have talked on the phone much more than we have seen each other, but I am really drawn to your inner beauty. It is rare to find someone with both."

This was the most comforting statement anyone had said to Annie. It made her want him more. The first date ended with a light kiss at Annie's door.

On another date, at a night club, Dmitri asked Annie to take a picture with him. She was dressed in hot pants with knee high boots. He kept a picture and gave her one. Due to their busy schedule, they saw each other once a week; but talked on the phone every day. Each time they met, their kisses got longer and more passionate. She gave all her tongue to his warm and firm kisses.

Again, Annie was in a situation similar to the last relationship with Kenny; a perfect man with ambition; who liked her and her child; but wanted children.

The difference was Dmitri was not in a hurry. He was only two years older than Annie and there was a lot he wanted to accomplish; as did Annie. He encouraged Annie to go back to school and to obtain a degree.

After three months of dating, Dmitri took Annie to a night club that was not officially opened. The outside entrance was very nice; it had a long walk way to the front door; a small porch and a grassy area. The inside had a very

**236**

large dance floor with a disco décor. It was decorated with booth tables and small four seated tables with glass candles on them. The large bar seated about twenty people. The place was very colorful with black and red accents. Annie saw no one in the place except her and Dmitri. He escorted Annie to a table and pulled out a seat for her. Annie sat down. Someone came from the back of the place with a tray that had sparkling apple cider and two glasses. The waiter poured the cider into the champagne glasses. Dmitri raised his glass.

"Annie I just want you to know how much I appreciate you. You deserve so much. I like everything about you. This is a special time for me. Please raise your glass and share with me a toast to my new club."

Annie was so surprised and happy for Dmitri. She gave congrats to him and kissed him. Dmitri got up to turn on music and he played, Roberta Flack, "The first time ever I saw your face".

Dmitri held out his hand for hers and pulled her close to him as they danced. Annie felt like a true princess for the very first time. He kissed Annie so deep and passionately that every inch of her desire was on fire. She wanted him then. They continued to dance and grin and kiss. He rubbed his groins against hers and they held it there for that satisfying moment. Annie could feel Dmitri's hardness against her. She held on tight giving it back and kissed him with all her tongue. Annie heard the music lyrics:

"And the first time ever I kissed your mouth I felt the earth move in my hand."

Then she felt him tighten up squeezing her so tightly- hollering her name "Annie". He eased the hold, breathing hard.

"Oh Annie, I wanted this to be perfect. I held it in for so long. I'm sorry."

Annie didn't mind, she felt loved.

"It was special; and you make me feel very special to you," she told Dmitri.

"I'm glad, because you are." He kissed Annie again and excused himself.

When Dmitri returned, he sat down with Annie.

"The club will open on Thursday, but the big open house will be Saturday night. I want you here with me on Saturday."

"I wouldn't miss it." Annie said.

Annie was excited that Dmitri asked her and she looked forward to the event.

The next few days Annie felt like she was on clouds. Although she spoke to Dmitri every day, she couldn't wait to see him. Five days felt like forever.

Valencia was elated for Annie's happiness and said she would attend the opening with her. Valencia offered to drive just in case Annie decided to go home with Dmitri.

Annie dressed up in a mini skirt with a strapless top and a pair of platform heels. She styled her hair in a curly style and wore large hoop earrings. Dmitri seemed to like her in that style. He had told her how much he liked looking at her "fyne" legs and her thin waist.

When Annie and Valencia drove up to the place, there were many people standing in the grassy area and on the porch area. Annie didn't see Dmitri right away, but she and Valencia stopped to talk with some of the people they already knew. About a half hour later it was getting dark. Annie saw Dmitri walking towards her. He made a brief stop to say something to a person and continued to walk towards her. He smiled and she smiled back. When he approached her he kissed her.

"Hey Love, so glad you are here. You look so beautiful. Let's go inside."

He guided Annie to the front door. Someone standing at the door opened it. Annie felt Dmitri let go of her arm to let her inside first. So she kept walking. Just as she entered the thrush hole, the door slammed closed behind her. Annie looked back, but Dmitri wasn't behind her. She thought maybe he had stopped to talk with someone. The club was full inside, so Annie took a seat at the first available table to wait on Dmitri. Within moments Valencia came in running.

"Annie, Annie, come with me, he's been shot."

Annie in disbelief, walked outside with Valencia. Dmitri was lying near the door on the ground with blood coming from his back. He did not move – a man kneeled over him to talk to him, but Dmitri did not respond. Annie stood there; could not move, but watched. The police and ambulance were there in minutes and they told everyone to get back. The med checked Dmitri's vitals and lifted him onto a stretcher and into the ambulance.

"Do you want to ride in the ambulance with him, Annie?" Valencia asked.

"No, please drive me to the hospital."

When Annie arrived in the hospital emergency area, there were several people waiting for Dmitri's diagnosis. A few of his

**240**

family members were there when the doctor came
out and announced:

"Dmitri is dead."

Annie took off running and Valencia
followed her. She didn't catch up with Annie
until they reached the car. Valencia unlocked
the car doors and Annie jumped in.

"What if that bullet was meant for me,
instead of him? This can't be. Did I cause
this? Poor Dmitri!!" Annie cried out.

# CHAPTER 58

*Forward To Present 2014*

With tears streaming down her face, sixty-four year old Annie held on to the picture of Dmitri and her. She stared at his stunning eyes and smile as she thought about what could have been between them. She wondered why someone would take the life of such a loving person.

Annie believed that if the bullet was intended for her, that there was only one person who would want her dead, Floyd. She had to get her child and herself to safety.

# CHAPTER 59

*Resolution*

Annie stayed in the house all day Sunday trying to figure things out. Weeks before, she had been getting a few hang up phone calls and thought a couple of times someone was following her. She couldn't eat and she couldn't sleep thinking about Dmitri.

The next morning when Annie arrived at work, she pulled out Ralph Carter's business card; the Executive Director of the San Francisco Division. Annie called his office and told his secretary that he had asked her to call about an important matter. She got through to him. Annie could tell that Carter had a little problem remembering her. But, she asked if he had any job openings that she could start right away. Carter told Annie he would call her back in a couple of days.

The next call was to Annie's mother. Annie asked her mother for her sister's (Aunt Olivia) phone number in San Francisco. Margaret gave it to her. Annie didn't give Margaret the details about what had happened, but told her that she had to move.

"I will call your Aunt Olivia to let her know you are coming," Margaret told Annie.

**243**

Annie didn't wait for returned calls before she submitted her job resignation and gave a notice of termination to her landlord. She packed her car with as many personal items as she could and had them shipped to San Francisco. She gave away and donated all her furniture and made airplane reservations for two.

Within one week, Annie's two best friends, Kenny and Valencia, with little Lena, drove up in front of Annie's house to take her and Whitney to the airport. Tears flowed from all eyes. No one knew when or if they would see one another again. Annie's friends waved goodbye as she and Whitney were on their way to an unknown future on the west coast.

Annie held little Whitney closely beside her on the airplane headed to San Francisco, as she prayed;

"Lord, build a fence all around me, and protect me as I travel on my way!"

**THE END**

# OTHER WORKS BY THE AUTHOR

## are on the following page

*Historical Fiction Drama*

**Middle Child 2: Better Than Good.** Annie moves to the west coast, where she is faced with difficulties in balancing her career choices and single parenting. More dangerous pursuers, undermining perpetrators, and financial hardship-- all become life's lessons learned before she could soar into a new world of her own.

**Sold on  Amazon, Kindle, Books A Million, Barnes & Noble**

# AUTHOR'S SHORT STORIES

### *Family Historical Fiction*

**Middle Child Short Stories Untold: Annie's Diary Series.** This collection of family-historical-fiction short stories is based on true stories beginning in the mid-1950s. The series is an extension of the author's novels, ***"Middle Child: Build a fence all around me"***, *and **"Middle Child 2: Better than good",*** and consists of inspiring untold stories that are appropriate for all readers.

**Sold on Amazon - Paperback and Kindle**

# AUTHOR'S FAMILY DRAMA NOVEL

## *Family Drama/ Romance/ Mystery*

**Logline:**  A young teacher struggles to be with her dying father while    evading her devious stepmother's deadly schemes.

**Synopsis:**  Maggie, a humble young elementary teacher, and only child of a business tycoon, learns that her father is dying. Her efforts to be with him become problematic as her jealous and deranged stepmother, Jennifer, plans deadly schemes against her. Maggie finds

**247**

support through unsuspected friendships and a love interest.

**Pitch:**     Part fable and modern reality, that weaves wealth, danger, betrayal, and fantasy into a richly satisfying tale, all framed with original songs.

**Sold on 2 Amazon - Paperback and Kindle**

# TEXTBOOK
## Professional Development for Pre-Professionals
## For All Majors and Careers

An educational resource for secondary and postsecondary education. The goal is to present one possible solution that meets the needs of individuals in determining and pursuing any career. Therefore, this textbook targets secondary and post-secondary education students interested in any fields including *Business, Education, Engineering, Legal, Medical, Performing Arts, and other areas.* Topics, group activities, and exercises include:

*Professional Behavior and Etiquette; Oratorical Skills and Techniques; Professional Guest Forums; Improving Interview & Audition Skills; Self-Image; Pros and Cons of Social Media. And Much More.*
**Sold on Amazon - Paperback and Kindle**

# POETRY

## Memoir

**FAMILY AND FAITH POETRY**
*Family Does Matter*

**TAJ SHOTWELL**
BESTSELLING AUTHOR WHO WROTE THE "MIDDLE CHILD" ANTHOLOGIES, COMING-OF-AGE IN MEMPHIS.

**An inspirational memoir of life's journey through fifty dramatic and loving short stories/poems over several generations, based on historical experiences about relatives and friends from Taj's historical**

hometown, Orange Mound, located in the southeast part of Memphis, Tennessee. Some poems address spiritual expressions and views, thoughts about international issues and communal societies, the complexities of families, (nuclear structured or otherwise), and confirm the family does matter. Many delightful photos are included.

## About the Author

# Taj Shotwell

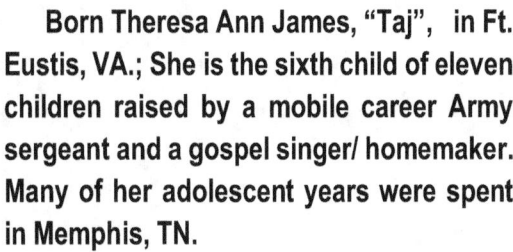

Born Theresa Ann James, "Taj", in Ft. Eustis, VA.; She is the sixth child of eleven children raised by a mobile career Army sergeant and a gospel singer/ homemaker. Many of her adolescent years were spent in Memphis, TN.

A retired, fully honored, university professor of business and educational leadership-- Dr. Shotwell published several educational research articles and a textbook. She earned a bachelor's degree in accounting and a master of business administration degree in international and multinational business from the Golden Gate University; and a doctorate in educational leadership from the University of San Francisco. Dr. Shotwell enjoys a healthy life style as a certified aerobic and fitness instructor; and taught dance fitness classes at various gyms, churches and centers throughout the USA and internationally. Dr. Shotwell greatest ambition, to develop a high school boarding school for performing artist with a unique concept, is in the making. She is an aspiring screenwriter, playwright, song lyricist, poet, and novelist. Beside the three part series of Middle Child, Dr. Shotwell is the author of a fictional family drama stage play and screenplay entitled, "Maggie: Never Bitter" and produced in Chicago. She wrote 16 songs for the musical. Sold on iTunes and all can be heard on YouTube. Wrote nonfiction books called "Profession Development for Pre-professionals in all Majors" and Family and Faith Poetry". Dr. Shotwell has a daughter and two grandchildren.